Arabella

Arabella Augusta Lousia were the imposing names which the Minister had just conferred on the golden-haired child in his arms. She gazed at him with some surprise in her huge violet eyes wondering why he had just poured water over her head.

The priest returned the child to her mother and, the baptism concluded, the Revd. Arthur Timson and his wife accompanied the small party to the nearby estate cottage where a splendid tea awaited them.

The ham was carved and served with pickles, salads and pies, together with wafer-thin bread and butter and copious cups of tea, for it was a warm summer's day.   The trifles and sweetmeats followed and then with some ceremony the Christening cake, which was most beautifully decorated, was cut.   Arabella's health was toasted with modest glasses of sherry.

This done, the Revd. and Mrs Timson departed.   They were soon followed by Mrs Simpson the cook and cake maker together with Miss Shields the lady's maid who left to return to their duties at Courtneys, where Arabella's mother Evelyn had served for nearly 30 years.

Having enjoyed the tea from her high chair Arabella was put to bed rather earlier than usual after her exciting day.

Her Godmothers Aunt Celia and Aunt Alice tidied away and soon Celia was collected by her husband and three younger children. Celia was always a busy farmer's wife whose four children and many animals kept her forever on the run. They were always hungry, and the slices of christening cake were soon eaten before they all left, waving happily from the pony and trap.

Seated opposite each other silence fell between the two sisters. Both had much to think of. At length Alice asked the question which had remained unspoken since her arrival from London the previous day.

She had brought with her the most wonderful christening robe of satin overlaid with lace and with intricate embroidery. Evelyn would lay it carefully aside to keep it for Arabella's children's christening.

Alice was a seamstress whose elegant work, practicality and sound common sense saw her in high demand as a dresser in the main London theatres. She stoutly resisted the many offers to attach herself to an individual artist permanently. By the time they had completed their season she had learned enough of their demands and tantrums to smilingly wish them well and wave them on their way.

Her skills ensured that Arabella's layette and all her childhood clothes were of the finest quality.

'Well, have your heard from Sean?' she asked, referring to Evelyn's absent husband.
The look of distress on her sister's face was enough to tell her the answer. 'No not a word, nor shall I. He was far too flamboyant and worldly for me!"

The absent Sean had arrived at Courtneys with a commission to paint a mural in the large nursery.

Lady Cynthia wished the children to grow up with nature always before them. A woodland scene was conceived with a glade where children picnicked. All manner of birds, insects, butterflies and animals moved among the trees. Sean's sketches had been accepted, and he arrived to take up the task, which was expected to last for three months.

The dark-eyed curly-haired charming Irish man was readily accepted into the Courtneys household. He preferred to take his lunch and tea where he worked but joined the staff for their evening meal. Here his stories of life in Ireland and the many interesting visits he had made to ply his craft proved enthralling.

To his great surprise his romantic interest settled not on one of the pretty young housemaids but on the more mature and handsome figure of Evelyn Seymour. The housekeeper had first come to Courtneys aged 13 as an under maid and had worked her way up to her present eminent status respected for her calmness, fairness and capabilities. It was clearly stated that she never asked anyone to do a job, however menial that she was not able or willing to do herself.

Her absolute refusal to succumb to his flattery and attentions were irresistible and caused him to redouble his efforts. At length his persistence was rewarded. Evelyn was unused to male attention having always discouraged any possible suitors. Sean was allowed to walk her home to her cottage for she 'lived out' except when the family were entertaining.

Soon he was stealing a goodnight kiss, and then invited in for a cup of hot chocolate. All further liberties were firmly refused despite Evelyn's high colour and trembling heart. Again to his total surprise he found himself proposing marriage and was swiftly accepted.

The Courtneys were to visit relatives in Scotland, so that Evelyn and Sean were able to marry by special licence with her two sisters as witnesses. Alice provided a delightful dress and jacket in pale green moire silk for the bride. The faithful Mrs Simpson and head housemaid, Margaret Smith, were guests. Bride and groom hosted a splendid lunch at a pleasant hotel.

The guests departed and Evelyn was tenderly introduced to the secrets of married life by her ardent groom. She proved to be an adept pupil. The couple returned to Courtneys following their three day honeymoon well contented.

Sean was asked to stay on at Courtneys to work on the bedroom corridors. Thus it was that when he moved on to Scotland for his next commission he left behind a blooming bride who was two months pregnant.

They parted with his many protestations of affection and the promise to write most regularly and to visit whenever possible. In reality he breathed a sigh of relief. The reality of an older wife with the prospect of a child to form a further responsibility, were not for him.

Somehow he never did tell Evelyn of his new address, wrote only twice and never visited her. Despite her despair Evelyn told no-one of her worries and was completely fit during her pregnancy. As she approached both her seventh month and 42nd birthday she requested a meeting with Lady Cynthia. To her she confided the truth of her position. Could she perhaps track him down through the Scottish relatives?

The answer when it came was devastating. Sean had completed his commission, and with his fee paid to him had decamped together with the second housemaid! He had promised her a visit to Ireland where she fully expected that they would be married.

Faced with his mendacity and with the promise of Lady Cynthia's discretion , Evelyn retired to her cottage. This had been the hugely generous wedding gift from Sir Charles and Lady Cynthia for her hollow marriage. There she awaited the birth of her child, with Alice to take leave from her job in London to attend her.

It was no surprise to that lady that with so much worry and despair, just as her sister's pregnancy had been so easy so her delivery was to prove nearly fatal.

Only the skill of Dr. Benson saved her as she battled not only a breach birth but a huge haemorrhage. As she struggled for life her baby was so perfect as to astonish all who saw her.

Drawing on every reserve of her strength, Evelyn determined that her perfect daughter should not be left without a mother as well as with an absent father. Gradually she pulled through with Alice's constant care, who though never having had a child herself, was adept at meeting the baby's needs.

Aunt Celia and the Courtneys' cook ensured that nourishing food was provided daily for the little household.

It had taken almost a year before Evelyn had felt able to arrange the christening and now spend this quiet time with her sister.

'I must get back to work very soon, Alice. My savings are depleted and I know that you used much of yours during the months that you looked after us

Lady Cynthia, had of course, appointed a replacement housekeeper. I have two interviews set up. One is with a vicar who is a widower with two young children and would accept Arabella. The other is for an unmarried lady who writes very sternly of her requirements with many rules. Arabella could accompany me but would need to be minded, so that I would only see her when I was off duty. Only Lady Cynthia's glowing references have earned me these interviews, and both are less than ideal positions'.

'Try not to worry' counselled her sister. ' You have overcome so much, have a very special child and with your good sense will win through'.

Alice returned to London the next morning to resume her job as a dresser at the Haymarket theatre.

Answering a knock at her door, Evelyn was surprised to see Lady Cynthia, who when seated quite suddenly burst into tears which she tried to wipe away with a scrap of lace handkerchief. Handing her former mistress a sensible cotton one, Evelyn offered comfort with a speedy tray of tea and some of her special sweet biscuits. Much restored, her ladyship hastened to share her problems.

'Everything is going wrong and I can't seem to restore matters. The maids quarrel and scrimp on their work. Nothing glows or shines, no fresh floral displays, just tired dry ones. Because the maids are unhappy the footmen are unsettled. Even cook is often behind with the meals. Sir Charles has complained that the weekend party was not a success, and had noticed the untidy hearths and poor fires. It is all so upsetting and I can think of only one solution. Instead of applying for a position elsewhere, I ask you to return to Courtneys. I will pay Mrs. Bishop one month's salary in lieu of notice and she can leave tomorrow with fair but not glowing references. We have important guests in two weeks and that barely gives you time to recover the situation. I beg you to say yes Mrs. Seymour.'

Mrs. Seymour was only too delighted to accept, but needed to discuss the care for Arabella, which would leave her free to do so.

Her ladyship had a ready solution to the problem. She suggested that Arabella should join her own children in the Courtneys nursery.

With Master Richard aged four and with Miss Caroline aged two, Arabella aged one should fit in well.

Evelyn had only two requests: The first of these that she be allowed to see her daughter each day during her afternoon break. The second that she – in other words Aunt Alice provide all

Arabella's clothing.

Evelyn's usual Sunday half day to allow her to attend church and to sing in St Bart's choir would continue.

Lady Cynthia left much relieved, and Evelyn felt extremely thankful at the happy resolution to her problems.

Her return to her former post was low key, as she greeted each maid and handed our their work schedules. Cook perked up now that she could discuss her problems and menus with her friend before presenting them to Lady Cynthia for approval.

Evelyn and Henry Ransome, the butler, agreed to hold a meeting to list all the work needed to bring Courtneys back up to pristine condition. His agreement and strong support stiffened her resolve to see the house and its residents returned to their former comfort. Top of her list was proper cleaning, with sparkling mirrors and hearths and lots of the fresh flowers and foliage arrangements at which she excelled.

For Arabella growing up in the Courtneys' nursery life was ruled by the routine of each day, and by the seasons. She grew to love Nanny Brown and the nursery maids, Ivy and Clara. Her mother delivered her into their care before breakfast each day.

Mornings were filled with play and lessons and there were toys of every sort from toy forts to a collection of wonderful dolls' houses. She and Caro spent endless hours re-arranging the toy furniture and playing with the dolls. Richard was usually to be found astride the largest rocking horse.

Lessons were informal as the girls were so young but progressed with their ages. Master Richard was idolized by both girls and by the staff. He often found Bella's huge violet eyes fixed on him.

Their nature walks allowed time for the children to explore the woods and the thrill of finding the first snowdrops and primroses in springtime was only equaled by the first chestnuts in autumn.

Each afternoon, while the siblings took their after lunch nap, Arabella joined her mother in the housekeeper's room. Books played a huge part in their lives, together with walks in the vegetable garden and in the rose garden if the family were out. Cook always produced milk and biscuits to enjoy with the housemaids before she returned upstairs. Meanwhile Richard and his sister had been primped for tea with their parents and warned by Nanny to be on best behavior.

In this way Arabella grew to know all the staff and accepted that her life was indeed charmed in the most special way. The schoolroom became ever more important and her love of books saw her learning to read and write at an early age.

Lady Cynthia believed that girls should be as well educated as boys and insisted that the schoolmaster, who came each day, treat the children equally and set them work suitable for their ages.

All understood that after her 5th birthday Arabella would move to the village school. Because she had many friends at the church Sunday school, which she attended every week, Arabella was quite excited at the idea. It was to be an interesting and expansive time. But first she would enjoy her birthday!

The house had a solid beauty, which was mainly due to its golden stone, welcoming portico and low shallow steps, with tall chimneys and sweeping lawns – but principally to its perfect proportions.

The builders had known their business and their skills had produced a house whose design and symmetry delighted the eye and gladdened the hearts of the family and of their guests.

Courtney Chase had originated as a hunting lodge whose owner, James Courtney, bred horses and sold them to the local gentry for the universal pastime of hunting.

His stud became a centre for excellence until a particularly feisty mare produced a colt of such splendor that James Courtney determined to present it to the king.   His future was assured by his majesty's delight in the colt and his patronage. James went on to marry a local heiress and they used her money to build the present house, extend the stud and shorten the name to Courtneys.

The house glowed, the garden bloomed, their marriage was happy and the estate extended until their son, Hugo Courtney, inherited. Hugo quickly purchased a pack of hounds and set about establishing his own hunt.   The cachet of membership of a Courtneys hunt, which was on the chase every available hour followed by lavish entertaining, brought him 'Hail fellow' friends galore.

The drain on the estate, his neglect of the stud and the disapproval of his wife- for were there not plenty of more agreeable women available – failed to dampen Hugo's extravagance.

The stirrup cup and cake had been served and the hunt had clattered off. Lady Sophia sighed, and shivering in the cold and frosty air, hurried indoors to ensure the lunch would be ready to dispatch, and that dinner was in preparation. A deal of brandy would be drunk on such a cold day.

As she enjoyed her coffee there was a loud banging and soon a sombre butler admitted two mud – bespattered riders. Sophia knew at once what had happened. Collecting herself as she absorbed their news, she asked how her husband had died. His usually sure footed mount had slipped on an icy patch, dashing its rider to the ground and had then fallen on him crushing him.

The hunt was returning escorting Sir Hugo's body. He was placed on a plank door, which was carried into the Great Hall by six of their numbers. The remaining men and women formed a guard of honour. Inside the servants were lined up as the body was placed on a large table in the centre of the hall.

With her husband dead, Lady Sophia determined that this would be the last hunt to be held at her home.

Following the elaborate funeral and with her son still minor, she held a meeting of the estate manager and Hugo's lawyers. It confirmed her worst fears. Hugo had virtually drained all the money, and his heavy wagers on his steeplechase horses had further weakened the estate.

Sophia did not hesitate. Winning the support and sympathy of the gentlemen
present she ordered the sale of the hounds, also all of the horses except for two carriage horses, two hacks and the children's ponies. Kennel men and grooms would also go. The money realised was to be invested in the estate farms and the new industries that were sweeping England.

Her reforms worked and Courtneys was safe for the future generations. In time fine paintings and furnishings enhanced the golden house even more and its comfort and beauty were unrivalled.

The business acumen and determined investments of Sophia continued in her successors.   Marriages were advantageous and the number of resulting children happily kept to three.   Thus the ladies were never exhausted or lost to childbirth.

Life at Courtneys for both its owners and their servants was indeed pleasant and orderly.

The lie first took hold on Arabella's fifth birthday, and was never admitted. At her request her party was to be a picnic in the woodland glade so like the one in the nursery mural.

On a glorious afternoon the three children played hide and seek, tag and chased butterflies with their nets. Their tea was laid out on a white cloth and Ivy, Clara and Nanny were happy drinking tea with Arabella's mother. The sandwiches, jellies, cakes lemonade and ever more tea for the ladies were enjoyed. Edie brought out the birthday cake, which Bella was allowed to cut with Ivy's help.

They all sang 'Happy Birthday' and joined hands to circle Bella with 'Ring a Ring of Roses'. Richard, who thought he was far too mature for such childish games, presented her with a circlet of roses.

Tired but happy, the children returned to the nursery. Bella was to stay the night as there was a very important dinner party where her mother was on duty. Bella spotted a butterfly in the mural just like the one she had chased.

'It looks so real Ivy'
'Well, your father was a real hand as a painter, and we all thought a lot of him.'
'My father painted all that big picture?'
'That he did.'
'Then, where is he and why does he never visit me' asked the child anxiously?
'Well he can't dear, for he was lost at sea.'

16

Arabella had always been told that her father worked away and quietly believed that he would return one day. Now 'lost at sea' as shown in her story books meant that she never would meet her father – that he never would come to see her. Thus her birthday ended in a lie and utter sadness. Evelyn had not the heart to correct it for it may perhaps have been true. A ferry to Ireland had foundered at about the same time that Sean and his new love were to travel there. Who knew?

The autumn brought great changes. Master Richard went early to prep school, Arabella began to attend the village Board school. The plan for her to stay with a local family after school proved difficult as Evelyn was so often detained at Courtneys. At length it was agreed that Alice should leave her post in London and return to keep house for her sister and niece.

Her needlework and tailoring skills were soon in demand, and she taught sewing to the older girls in the school.

Evelyn blessed the day that she had taken Arabella to choir practice with her.
They had always attended Sunday service at St Bart's with those servants who were free to do so, but choir practice with Evelyn was special.

'Special' was a word which occurred to her mother regarding her daughter on many occasions. From the day of her birth Arabella was intended for greatness. She had the looks, the character and now the Voice.

Having sung all the nursery songs and the songs at school, where singing broke up the more serious lessons, she loved to sit quietly in church.

Bella watched the Choirmaster as he waved his arms at the singers. Sometimes he grew a little cross if they did not come in on time or made the same mistake again. Mr. Lovett was not a man to be trifled with, and Mr. Goss the organist watched through his little mirror anxiously for his cue.

Evelyn had a clear soprano voice, which she used too little. As the choir ran through 'All Things Bright and Beautiful' one Thursday evening, when they reached the chorus, a voice of such utter clarity and purity joined in. As if by common consent the choristers stopped singing and Mr. Lovett turned to see Arabella singing the well loved words.

Wasting no time he invited Arabella to sing a solo verse and then another. Her poise and confidence were unparalleled. So it was that Evelyn's daughter became the 'Special' soloist for church festivals and the competitions, which Mr. Lovett now felt confident to enter.

She also was the recipient of free music lessons. Evelyn's heart swelled with pride and love. Her golden child would grow into a singer of much fame for her wonderful voice would ensure it. How sad that Sean would never know the joy of hearing his daughter sing.

Arabella's life had moved on. She missed Richard and Caroline and Nanny and Ivy and Clara a great deal. However, her busy days at school playing with her friends in the summer evenings or snug in the cottage with her mother and Aunt Alice in the winter made for a happy life.

She had a consuming interest in nature nurtured by her playtimes in the woods and garden of Courtneys. Bella began to always carry a little satchel of sketch pad and pencils.

Her efforts were improving with practices and now she could capture the character of a bird as it cocked its head, or the velvety texture of a flower, but most of all she loved butterflies.

She knew of the great book of birds in old St Edward's library and longed to see it again. It was so precious that it was kept under a cover and only opened to show to the most important guests. Her mother called it the 'Audubon' book.

Arabella did not tell her mother of the day when Sir Edward had shown it to her, and knew that she was destined to see it again one day.

Richard returned to Courtneys for the long summer holiday in poor spirits. He was at fourteen mature physically. Tall and well made, handsome, with the confidence of good family and breeding he was never the less insecure.

Fond of riding his father had promised him a new horse. The chestnut proved to be amenable and lively. His morning ride set him up for the day, so that Charlotte and her friend staying for a few weeks were happy in his company.

The arrival of a tutor engaged by his mother was an unwelcome surprise. Richard's reports from Eton were not glowing. He excelled at most sports but his academic progress was patchy.

However the young American proved 'sparky' and extra tuition was both informative and entertaining. The two girls joined them for drawing lessons and nature rambles.

It was while he was out riding that Richard came upon Arabella. She was sitting on a tree stump totally engrossed in sketching a deer, which fled on hearing the horse.

Dismounting he approached the girl. Her clear gaze remained unaltered, and her luxuriant golden hair was still dazzling. Bella greeted him warmly and shyly showed him her drawing. As he looked through her sketchbook Richard saw her undoubted talent.

When he returned home he visited his mother and insisted that

Lady Cynthia send for her housekeeper. Mrs. Seymour agreed that Bella be invited to share in the tutor's drawing lessons.

Autumn saw them all back at their studies and Francis Grantley returning to America. Richard had basked in Arabella's hero worship.   Whilst preening a little, he dismissed her as an impressionable child. He was far too grown up to take notice!

Arabella knew that her position as a junior housemaid at Courtneys was pre-ordained. She could expect steady promotion, and to eventually succeed her mother as housekeeper. Yet somehow she felt that somewhere, sometime in the future, her music must come to dominate her life. So like her mother before her she stayed on at school. She helped with the younger scholars and had a way with the less able ones.

Story time was so special to them all – when they could imagine so many lovely things outside of their normal lives. Arabella always ended by singing them a lullaby so that they returned home calm and happy and content.

Her school employed a headmaster and two assistant teachers who all helped to expand her own knowledge and horizons.

Mr. Lovett, her choirmaster, had insisted that she learned to read music and was able to pitch any note or run of notes that he requested. Bella was to concentrate on her breathing and diction. Wisely he made no 'intervention' in her voice production or unrivalled feeling for the music.

As she physically matured so her already formidable depth and range intensified. Although her repertoire was restricted to church music she found that her Aunt Alice had an extended experience of theatre, and indeed music hall songs. Together they enjoyed many a sing-song together of an evening. Mr. Lovett would definitely not have approved!

At last, now a lovely fifteen year old, Arabella donned the Courtney summer uniform of an under maid. Her blue and white striped dress with apron and cap was comfortable and becoming.

She might have had two problems but what her mother had anticipated and forestalled.

The first was the attention of both male servants and more difficult male guests, who often 'tried it on' with pretty maids. No footman would wish to incur Mrs. Seymour's wrath so they became very protective of Bella.

To any male guest Arabella was to smile sweetly and mention that her mother was Lady Cynthia's housekeeper and would at once be informed of any improper advances and thence her Ladyship.

However Arabella did fall in love – utterly, completely and forever – with Courtneys itself!

As she learned her duties the very stones seemed to speak to her. She knew that it was fanciful, yet the family portraits were not dead to her. They had been living people, all part of the house's history and changing fortunes.

Every task must be completed to her very best and her eagerness was endearing. She 'lived in' and it was soon clear that no stories would ever be carried back to her mother. This might have been her second problem as the housekeeper's daughter, but Arabella was no 'tell tale'.

She was seldom temperamental, and in the colder months her

appetite for cleaning hearths and lighting fires at the crack of dawn was unusual and appreciated by the other maids who hated the task.

The never ending work that was needed to keep the great house running smoothly was helped by the fact that every maid servant should be able to
tackle any task.   Evelyn Seymour insisted on this.

Arabella particularly disliked her week in the laundry.   All that steam, boiling, rinsing, bleaching and blueing before the drying and ironing for a large household was backbreaking.

In contrast cleaning grates, dusting and polishing and running up and down stairs a dozen times a day were easy tasks.

Bella sallied forth each morning clad in a rough cotton coverall to protect her uniform, with her hair bundled under a cloth square, tied around her waist was a rope with one coarse, one medium, and one fine hard brush and tucked in were a coarse, a medium and a fine cloth.   Her bucket and wet cloth were to hand.

A young footman would remove the ashes from the main rooms. Following on Arabella cleaned out the rest with her brushes, keeping the fine brush for the delicate carvings on the fireplace surrounds. Kindling, coal and logs were all ready for her to start the fire. Her soft cloths polished the mantle and surrounds while her rough ones shone the fire irons. With a wipe of her damp cloth over the clean hearth she was ready to move on to the next one.

The girls laughed at her strange appearance and so did Arabella herself, but her speed and efficiency were unquestioned.

Breakfast, lunch and especially the servants' supper were always lively and full of laughter from the younger staff. Mr. Ransome could look stern and call for order but he knew that a happy servants' hall made for a happy household.

Summer brought delight with no fires to light and feed. Bella could spend more time in the garden with Mr. Finch the head gardener. He was always ready to explain the vegetables, fruits and flowers to her. He kept a journal of the seasons and crops, so that he could alter the number and types of seeds he purchased. He noted frosts, high winds, drought, rain and snow and all the vagaries of the English weather.

He lavished care on the rose garden, which Lady Cynthia adored. Knowing that roses were voracious feeders, he obliged them with loads of manure, seaweed, water and careful pruning. His secret desire was to raise a new variety to be called after himself. The 'Archibald Finch' had a ring to it.

Pruning and grafting became a ceremony and no basket of his splendid fruit and vegetables gave him as much pride as one perfect rose presented to her Ladyship.

It pained him greatly that his special grafted bushes refused to produce a new rose.

During the next three years Arabella kept her own journals. They were pale copies of her mother's, which went back for so many years. It never the less pleased her to know when each chimney was swept and what jobs she tackled for the big annual clean which took place whenever the family left on their annual holiday.

As she approached eighteen, Sir Charles was nearing his half century well contented. He ran a fine estate, which his father had handed over to him. This left Sir Charles free to immerse himself in his books. Lady Cynthia managed the household for her husband's comfort and their two children were thriving.

Richard had reached his majority celebrated by an ox roast for the whole estate with much drinking and dancing. Never the less his wife insisted that Sir Charles must celebrate his half century in fine style.

All was ready for the great day. Side tables stood along the great hall where the footmen, in handsome new livery of royal blue with buff collars and cuffs and double row of brass buttons, would be ready to serve champagne and fine wines.

Mrs Simpson with a specially hired assistant cook and her kitchen maids were in a fever of anticipation, but well prepared. The splendid buffet supper would delight both the eye and the palate and extra staff stood ready. The large birthday cake was on display and the ladies had their new gowns ready.

Gilt chairs were placed before a dais where the majestic grand piano stood in all its glory. The accompanist had taken a light lunch and had laid out his music ready for the rehearsal. Madame Bertrand, the famous soloist, was due to arrive soon for her rehearsal and then to rest in one of the guest bedrooms before her performance.

Lady Cynthia burst into her husband's study with Ransome the butler following close behind.

'She's had an accident and can't perform tonight. Oh Charles, without the entertainment it will be a disaster. We can't have just supper and dancing.'

A discreet cough announced their redoubtable butler was about to come to the rescue.

'Your Ladyship has the answer here. You have heard Arabella Seymour sing in church, at concerts and no doubt around the house. She will fill in quite admirably.'

'But is there time for her to rehearse and will she be able to carry it off?'

'Undoubtedly your Ladyship. Perhaps you could send for her aunt who can bring her music and dresses.'

'Do so at once, Ransome and send Arabella to me here immediately.'

The young maid presented herself with a composure and certainty, which re-assured her employers. They were struck by her great beauty and unusually vivid eyes.   These would surely impress their guests, for the enjoyment of her beauty would please as well as her singing.

Arabella explained that she had just one problem.   Most of her repertoire was from pieces of Holy music like the Messiah and Zadok the Priest.   She knew no operatic arias, but was confident that she had time with her own music and the easier pieces that Jasper Arlington, the accompanist, had brought that they could produce an enjoyable entertainment.   They would also include some popular songs of the day and perhaps the guests would join in.   This suggestion caused Lady Cynthia to raise her eyebrows for they were Courtneys not some common music hall.

'Just do your best my dear' she said and Arabella dashed off to begin her rehearsal but found it was harder to agree the programme than she had thought.   An unlikely inspiration arrived in the form of her Aunt Alice, who had heard so very many performances from the wings of London theatres that she instinctively knew what would 'take'.

She said to start with the classy stuff, then move to serious parlour songs. Next a more popular section and close with a quite sentimental section. Final with a rousing song but Arabella insisted that she would finally sing a lullaby.

Together Arlington and Bella addressed the technicalities and worked also on understanding each other's styles.   This established a rapport, which proved to be so valuable. Should the inexperienced Bella falter, then he would play a little louder and increase the tempo to help her recover.

'Increase – not slow down?'

'Indeed not – I find that gives both you and I the time and the audience does not notice.'

The rehearsal continued. Bella was warned not to sing at her full volume in order to conserve her voice for the performance. When they were both happy, especially with the entries, they took a break, after first ensuring that their music sheets were in order.

Arabella joined her Aunt in the small parlour, which had been converted into the dressing room. Here the contents of Alice's small trunk were revealed. She had an extensive collection of gowns mainly gifted to her during her 'dresser days'.

With some swift adjustments and the preparation of a passable dressing table all was ready. Arabella took frequent small sips of water but declined to eat anything.

So it was that by 9 o'clock the guests had all been greeted and well supplied with delightful champagne and wines. They had admired each other's dresses and chatted happily.

Invited to take their seats, they awaited the mature diva they knew was to appear. No announcement to the contrary had been made as Lady Cynthia was relying on the surprise element to assist Arabella.

There was a low murmur of interest as a beautiful young woman appeared. She wore the simplest of white Grecian style gown. It clung revealingly to her glorious figure accentuated by a fine golden cord under her pert bosoms.

She stood before them appraising her audience with her luminous violet eyes. Her golden hair cascaded over her shoulders, and she wore no gloves so that her rosy arms with their dimples showed to advantage.

The intro began and her melodic voice bathed them with its warmth and beauty.

No one present doubted that they were in the presence of a great and unique voice; a voice which would bring delight to all who heard it. Bella's control, range and depth were unusual in one so young, being already developed and mature.

They gloried in its beauty and were generous in their applause. Further into her performance Bella turned and took from a waiting chair a scarlet tunic and hussar's cap. There followed many rousing songs where her audience enthusiastically joined in. Then it was time for her only change of costume made while Jasper gave a virtuoso piano solo.

Bella reappeared wearing another delightful gown in the most delicate shade of lilac. Over her right shoulder was a spray of pale mauve to deep violet flowers, with a similar spray in the left side of her hair. This had been chosen by Alice to cleverly enhance Arabella's unusual eyes.

When the last note of her final lullaby faded away her audience rose as one and applauded her whole-heartedly. Bella bowed first to her accompanist then to each sides of her audience. She had been frugal in her gestures only using them to gracefully emphasise her high points. Now she acknowledged her audience with smiling waves, and with a final bow retired. No encore was requested or expected for the guests knew that the young singer had given her all.

Cook's buffet was admired, supper was enjoyed and the hosts congratulated on finding such an outstanding artist.

Sir Charles cut his birthday cake and received the toasts and good wishes of his friends and neighbours. In his modest speech he included Arabella and thanked her for stepping in and filling the breach.

The following day Lady Cynthia received a note from the Hon. Mrs. Richards. It thanked her for a most splendid party and contained a request. Would she approach Arabella with an invitation to sing at her son Christopher's coming of age party?

Thus did Arabella's rise to fame and fortune begin.

At Alice's insistence Arabella asked if she might invite a guest to her next engagement, Christopher's birthday party. In truth it was a London acquaintance of her Aunt's, a theatre impresario. He could not believe his luck in seeing the magical combination of such great beauty, such magnetism and such a magnificent voice.

Pure box office gold!

Bella had adjusted her programme to appeal to the younger people without antagonising their elders. During the finale she looked directly at Christopher – the birthday boy – and he fell hopelessly in love. Since the young man was determinedly non-romantic this great awakening amazed him.

He searched for her to take supper with him and hopefully to dance.

Aware that she was known to be Sir Richard and Lady Cynthia's housemaid, she felt it would be better if she slipped away with her Aunt. Leaving Richard to search in vain.

The fee which she had received at Julia Richards insistence seemed to Bella to be substantial. However her meeting with Mr. Davenport was sobering. On the plus side were her youth, beauty and staggering voice. However she was inexperienced and had a limited repertoire. She would need at least six months of constant study – perhaps longer – before she was ready to be launched at first national, and then international levels.

Her experienced Aunt would accompany her as companion, dresser and advisor.

Also Hugh Davenport insisted that she had her own lawyer to oversee her contract, and her own banker to manage the funds, which he knew would pour in. Meanwhile he must bear the costs.

Towards the end of six months' non stop whirl of meetings, singing lessons, costume fittings makeup lessons, deportment and stage presentation, he made Arabella one booking. This was in the very fashionable city of Bath. A benefit concert was to be given at the Assembly Rooms sponsored by a very wealthy widow.

If the unknown 'Arabella' could make her mark in front of such an influential and refined audience then the news of her would spread like wildfire.

In a full programme Bella would be allowed just four songs and was near to the bottom of the bill. The thrill of seeing her name on any bill was very special. He gown was of fluid silver fabric, which enhanced her alluring figure, with silver leaves in her hair.

Alice and Mr. Davenport agreed that to start with one of her newly learned arias would set the tone for her as a serious singer. After her final lullaby there was a long silence followed by muted applause.

This salutary lesson served to show Arabella that Alice was right, adding a rousing finale to her act left the audience energised and cheering for more.

While her French and Italian were improving German was indeed a foreign language. It was apparent that at least three more months' tuition was needed before Bella was ready.

Hugh Davenport had pioneered the idea of having three separate travelling trunks. Each held costumes, accessories and the music to be performed. Instead of the incessant packing and unpacking of one large trunk, the current one could be used at each venue. Also if one went adrift there would be no panic.

Only their personal clothing, a bag with makeup and music for Arabella and a wicker sewing basket for Alice needed to travel directly with them.

Now for Arabella's professional debut.

It was a bitter blow when my dear son Charles died in a shooting accident. He had willingly and effectively taken over the running of Courtneys. It was his sound management, which was helping us to avoid the pitfalls of the great agricultural depression. Ever ready to listen to advice and in a happy marriage with Cynthia, I was left to retire to the library and enjoy my large collection of books.

My grandson, Richard, was fit and strong if rather hot headed. By contrast his sister Caroline was quiet and sweet natured.

Their father had left Richard on a loose rein as he enjoyed the role of well to do heir to a reasonably sized estate. He was intended to work with the estate manager after he left university to learn the ropes. With sizeable farms, forestry, shooting parties, husbandry, tenancies, and keeping the account books there was much administration.

Richard managed to enjoy his visits to the farm. His easy manner with the farmers, their workers and their daughters made him popular. The Glorious Twelth could not come soon enough, replacing the hunting parties, which had never taken place at Courtneys since the days when Richard's ancestor Sir Hugo had died in the hunting field. Richard was a fine rider and again and again asked his father to host the local hunt without success.

To come into his inheritance at the age of 25 was unexpected, and inflated his self-importance and extravagance. His mother and I tried to remind him of his responsibilities. He treated his mother with scant respect and regarded me as a useless infirm old bore. Infirm at 78 years of age I may be, but boring – never!

Chapter 11 Richard 1901

The death of my Father came as a bit of a shock. He wasn't a bad old buffer and we rubbed along well enough. I knew that he was hugely fond of me and proud of my sporting achievements.

He never scolded me when I missed the everlasting meetings he ran with Jarvis, the estate manager. I was always far too busy, but never shirked those with his solicitor or the banker for obvious reasons.

I hoped that none of them knew of my amatory exploits. If the girls were up for it then so was I. They all knew that it was just a bit of fun. After all I did have a duty to marry well and quite fancied any heiress whose dowry would last me out.

As for Grandpa, Mama and Caroline, they could be dispatched to the Dower House when it suited me.

Meanwhile I had a hunt day to organise. I informed Mama and Cook that we should need stirrup cup and fruit cake, with lunch to be sent out to one of the lodges and a fine dinner served in the evening.

Mrs. Seymour was getting on a bit, but she knew her stuff, allocating bedrooms and such.

I haven't heard much about her famous daughter lately. What a beauty she was always ogling me with her great violet eyes. I look forward to meeting her again.
TALLY HO!

Anybody what's anybody knows as 'ow the gardens are a lot more special than the big 'ouse.

Here I am wi' two under gardeners and two lads. We works 'ard and produces loads o' grand fruit and veg. Cook wants 'er basket every day an 'Mrs. Seymour does 'er posh flower arrangements, but it's me as cuts the flowers and greenery an' sticks 'em in a bucket 'o cold water fust.

Her Ladyship loves the rose garden and' allus walking there. Ah'm everlastin' feedin an' prunin', while she might manage a bit o' gentle deadheadin'! She often tek's 'er mornin' coffee in the little pavilion there, so I 'as to watch out for 'er.

'Mr. Finch or Mr. Finch may I have a word?' So that 'll be another 'ours wok, an' just when it's time for me tea and biscuits.

Ah've allus kept a journal o' the seasons – what's growed an' what's not done so well. 'Ow many seeds an' varieties ah've bought, an the names and colours of all the bletherin' roses. And the weather o' course.

Still it's not a life to be sneezed at. Fact is, ah niver does git the sneezes. It must be all the fresh air an' an apple, pear or plum when ah fancies one.

Either that or it's sniffing all the blasted roses wi' her Ladyship.

NOW WHERE'S ME TEA AN BISCUITS

'I can't really believe that after so long and learning so much I am at last to embark on a London season'. So mused Bella as she applied her stage makeup. Just enough to enhance your own colouring and good looks under the lights – no overload,' the macquilist had advised. 'Let's point up your eye colour which is so unusual and emphasise your lips. Most of the audience will be concentrating on your face, though not all with a figure like yours.'

Her new accompanist was a lively Irishman who was quite flashy in his solo pieces but also a clever and supportive accompanist. The two roles are very different. They had a good affinity, which was absolutely essential. The final rehearsal had gone well – not at full volume of course to conserve Arabella's voice.

Now Aunt Alice was ready with her gown of shot gold silk and would fix her hair ornament. Soon she would kiss Bella at the side of the stage, which she must remember to call the wings. The shawl would be slipped from her shoulders and she would hear 'Break a leg my dear'.

The stage manager gestured that she was on. The thrill of it all chased away the butterflies for she had worked long and hard for this moment.

She gazed out, took her cue from 'Fitz' and launched into her great opening aria.

I had long ago changed from nursery maid to housemaid, Nanny and Rosie had moved on when Master Richard and Miss Caroline no longer needed them.

When I told Bella about her Dad after her birthday party, I could have bit me tongue off. Mrs. Seymour had always warned us to tell the child that her Pa was away and then I goes and lets out that he had been lost at sea. If Mrs. Seymour had wanted her to know she'd have told her herself when Bella was older.

At least it seems to have blown over now and Bella is the toast of London. Them toffs can't get enough of her grand voice. Mrs. S reckons they wait for ages to get tickets to hear her. She'll be off all over Britain then to foreign parts. Everybody has heard about her now.

She's in the papers an' all and Mrs. S showed us her photo looking ever so smart and smiling like an angel.

Just think, that little baby that I looked after and now she's famous.

It'd be good if Mr. Richard 'ud settle down. He's 25 now and sending Lady Cynthia mad with worry at his wild ways. Cook and Mrs. S only stay on because they care about Lady Cynthia and Miss Caroline.

When I found out that scheming old man had colluded with my father to block my inheritance I went mad I think.

Calling for Raven to be saddled, I rode until neither of us could go a step further.

I walked him back to the village inn and stabled him there.   Then I threw some sovereigns on the bar and drank until I passed out.

They sent up to Courtneys and I woke up in my own bed, with a terrible hangover and an even more terrible all consuming rage.

My allowance would never cover my needs.   I need money to entertain my friends, for more horses, for grooms and for wagering.   Then there are the cards and my conquests.

They may have blocked me from selling off any part of the estate but I've still got the house and all its contents.

First to go will be my Grandfather – and his library!

Life at Courtneys has changed so much since Richard inherited and not in any good way.

He was enraged and shouted and used the foulest language when he found that Sir Charles and Sir Edward had appointed three trustees to oversee the estate until he reaches the age of thirty-two.

He is unable to sell any part of the estate without their consent. I can only think that they mistrusted him to manage things properly. Even his increased allowance doesn't satisfy him

He ignores his Grandfather, belittles his Mother and bullies Miss Caroline.

Poor Mr. Ransome has his choice of wines questioned and the valet is in despair too.

Only cook still has a soft spot for her ' Master Richard' but even she is sorely tested when he brings back his cronies for meals without warning. When they arrive shouting and demanding wine, the mistress and Miss Caroline join Sir
Edward in the library. I know that Lady Cynthia wants them all to move to the Dower House soon. Cook and I will get them settled there and then we can both retire.

I hate to see the mess that Richard and his guests leave for us to clean up. The maids are up in arms and have threatened to leave too.

At least the news of Alice and my dear Arabella is wonderful!

Now I understand why I knew that she was born to be famous.

At the back o' me garden journal I writes the words o' the songs I sing to mysen' as I works or else they'll be lost. And not always to messen neither.

I reckons that if ah'd sung a duet wi' that saucy maid Arabella at Sir Charles's birthday party, ah'd 'hve finished up, in London, an got famous an' all.   It'd be 'Goodbye' to the danged roses an' slavin in this 'ere garden.   Ah might get 'er ma to send 'er me songs, then she can use 'em, and pay for them an' all.

She'll be away to Pairs, Vienna, Rome and Venice and Mrs. S says she's booked for America next.   All them places ah'll niver git to see. My, she sang grand at the Master's birthday, but it's the cake ah'l remember.   Good luck to the lass anyroad.

Ah've 50 roses in me journal an' most of 'em ave shades of red or pink.   Now 'er Ladyship wants 5 more varieties getting.

Damn and blast the roses!   Ah lost interest when me graftin' an pollinatin' never cum up to scratch.

Ah'm still waitin' for a FINCH ROSE

Two years after inheriting Courtneys Richard made good his threat. Without warning a gang of men arrived to strip out the library.

Sir Edward's cherished books, first editions included, were all boxed up to go to London for auction. Sir Edward sat at his desk and watched it all somberly. Ransome appeared with a glass of brandy then Mrs. Seymour brought in his coffee herself

He sat unmoved stricken by the actions of his Grandson. It had been bad enough to lose his agreeable son – now this! At least they left his great Audubon Book of American Birds untouched on its stand and under its cover. Even Richard hesitated to remove such a treasure.

At length he rose, moved across, removed the cover and opened this wonderful folio. Each page was large and heavy, made of linen paper. The glories they revealed were now world famous and recognised as the work of a very special naturalist. Every species was shown totally realistically. They had been shot then wired onto a chequered board in realist posed before being drawn on to chequered linen paper. Thence they were coloured in crayon and watercolour.

John James Audubon had been an adventurer, hunter, naturalist and artist. He was of French parentage but was sent to help manage the family's American estates as a young man. Commerce did not interest him, but the huge numbers of birds did. He was amazed at their variety and shot them in their hundreds He married a young English woman but left repeatedly for expeditions down the east coast. His first thousand drawings left in a chest had been eaten by rats so he started again, determined to do even better.

Having run through the money from the sale of the family estates, he and his wife faced poverty, but nothing could stop him as he continued with his 'Great Work'. He continued to shoot skin and paint all the new species he found and they were so lifelike they appeared to fly off the pages.

Audubon actually included up to 440 pages and sold them by subscription, finding good engravers and painters in England.

At the final page, Sir Edward closed the folio sat down at his desk, took a sip of brandy. Then he surveyed his ravaged library and simply died.

He had directed that only his family, tenants, estate workers and staff were to attend his funeral at St Bartholomew's. This was to be followed by a modest reception with only a toast and NO speeches.

Thus this true gentleman 'shuffled off this mortal coil' and joined his ancestors in the Courtney family vault.

Finch never did have to plant more roses. Immediately after Sir Edward's funeral, Lady Cynthia and Miss Caroline moved to the Dower House.

Their ladies' maid, Mrs. Seymour, cook one housemaid and one kitchen maid moved with them.

Ransome was left to find a new cook and to manage Courtneys as best he could.

Arabella received the news of Sir Edwards's death with great
sorrow. She had honoured him for his extensive knowledge and
scholarship. Only her mother would now remember Bella's bond
with her old master.

It all happened one particularly lovely July summer day in 1897.
The family had left for an extended holiday. Footmen and maids
rose early and worked well under Mr. Ransome and Mrs.
Seymour's supervision. They were allowed tea in the garden and
extra beer and cordial with their supper. A hearty lunch kept
them going.   This was spring cleaning on a grand scale.

Arabella asked her mother to be allowed to tackle Sir Edward's
library. She would need the help of a footman to climb up and
dust the fretwork along the top of each bookcase. Then she
needed about eight books removed from one end of each of the
top three shelves. She also needed the rest to be moved along
and dusted back into position before the end eight were replaced.

Once this was completed she could manage the rest herself. The
gloomy old velvet curtains were removed. Mrs. Seymour's
journals told her of their age and that they were overdue for
replacement. She decided boldly to use golden brocade.

Arabella assumed a cotton wrapper and tied up her hair. She had
two soft brushes and two light dusters and began working
relentlessly. Each day saw her handling the books with extreme
care. First a soft brush then a delicate cloth to burnish their
bindings before they were moved back along a shining shelf. She

did not confront the extent of her task – but just kept moving methodically on.

On what would be her last day the new curtains were hung at shining windows while matching cushions graced the library chairs. Arabella stepped outside, removed her overall, shook out her hair, and from the rose garden plucked one perfect golden rose for Sir Edward's desk.

Arabella has saved the crowning moment until now. She reverently removed and folded the cover, then opened the great Audubon book. Its' beauty overwhelmed her. She turned the magnificent pages until she came to a Golden Eagle. As she gasped at its glory she failed to hear the door behind her open.

At length a quiet voice said 'So you are the young lady to whom I owe my sparkling library.' Gravely he took the rose from its vase and presented it to Arabella with a bow. Then he walked to the door, opened it for her and bowed again.

No words were needed or exchanged. Both knew that their love of books and beauty was shared.

The news of Sir Edward's death was followed by a letter, which reached her in Boston from her London lawyers. It informed her that Sir Edward Courtney had left her a legacy, which she was to collect from Courtneys when she was next in England.

Arabella had been almost permanently on tour for three years. Her Aunt was tired and the new maid who now travelled with them was cheerful and capable.

A return to England was certainly overdue. Arriving safely in Southampton, the three ladies took a train to London where Bridie was to remain with friends.

Bella was surprised at the unkempt state of the steps when she arrived at Courtneys. She rang the great doorbell, which she had polished so often.
Her mother had warned her, but the sight of a disheveled maid with cap awry rather than a liveried footman was another surprise.

Giving her name she watched as the slovenly maid gaped before she ushered Bella in and led her towards to the library. 'Thank you, I know the way', dismissed the girl. The walls of the great hall had many empty spaces. Arabella saw with despair the Knellers, Gainsboroughs, Reynolds and Romneys were gone.

She knocked lightly on the heavy library door and entered.

There he sat florid and a little untidy in his dress with a glass at his elbow. Richard rose to his feet, seated her, offered her coffee and then openly inspected her.

He saw a young woman of twenty-three with great assurance and presence. She was fashionably and expensively dressed in a travelling costume with her abundant hair neatly styled under an elegant hat. Here was the girl he remembered yet somehow that innocence was now cloaked in a veneer of success and fame.

She greeted him politely and handed him the lawyer's letter informing her of Sir Edward's bequest, and a further assurance one to authorize her to collect it.   He saw her immediately notice the absence of the great Stubbs painting over the mantelpiece and the empty bookshelves.

Tossing the letters aside, he directed Arabella to the stand where the uncovered Audubon folio lay, for this was her legacy. Bella was overwhelmed that Sir Edward had seen the look of awe on her face and had decided that she would treasure his gift as beyond rubies. Approaching the stand she felt the first stirrings of unease. The great book held 400 pages and usually stood proud. Now it appeared to be flat and diminished.

As Bella reached to open it, she knew at once what Richard had done. Inside were neatly cut edges where the great paintings had been removed. Perhaps only eighteen remained. She turned on him with such a look of contempt and icy rage that he took a step back, and an ugly flush suffused his neck and face.

'What a pathetic excuse for a man you have become Richard. Stealing indeed but to ruin one of the world's great works of art is beyond comprehension. Keep it!'

With that Arabella stalked to the door.   She felt slivers of ice pierce her heart as she saw what had become of her beloved Courtneys. So much beauty lost to one man's greed and weaknesses. He must have had huge gambling losses to use up so many of Courtneys treasures and resources.

Her mother had told her that when the Paul Storr silver went then so did Mr. Ransome.   All had deserted him.

His voice pursued her down the hall.   'The old fool shouldn't have left it to you anyway.   It is my inheritance!'

It had been such a joy to have my dear Arabella back home with Alice too.   Under her veneer of fame and sophistication she is still my darling girl.   I delight in her worldly success, but also that beneath it all she remains so kind and modest even.

We had such a lovely week together.   She took us out to the farm to see Celia, Fred and her cousins.   So much laughter, shrieks of delight and such excitement to see Bella.   I know that she enjoyed being back with her family again.

She put aside her fancy clothes and wore the summer dresses, which I'd kept from before she left us.   Bella did dress up to go and visit Lady Cynthia and Miss Caroline.   She returned very quiet indeed.   Alice managed to find out why.   Bella had found her Ladyship much aged, and Caroline pale and unwell.

Knowing that it would distress them to talk about Courtneys, she had told them of her travels, of the great cities, which she had visited, and the splendid concert halls where she had performed.

Lady Cynthia could not help speaking of Bella's first performance at her dear late husband's birthday party.   What a splendid and happy evening it had been for them all.   In fact it seemed to her to be the last happy event she could remember.

How she and Caroline missed Sir Charles and Courtneys and their lives there together.   She spoke wistfully of the lovely rose garden, which she had established.   She longed for those days to be back and she knew that FINCH missed her too.

I did not quite understand why Bella asked me to send a note by one of the village boys to John Jarvis the agent, asking him to visit us and to slip in after dark.   Why does she need to see the estate manager so secretly?

Alice, Arabella and I attended St Bart's on Sunday.   The minister, choirmaster and organist have all retired.   Bella had a word with Revd. Peters, and Sidney Jameson the new organist.   Without rehearsal she stood up and sang "I Know That My Redeemer Liveth'.   I can never describe the wonder of her magnificent voice filling St. Bart's.   The feeling of reverence and joy washed over us all.

Everyone wanted to speak to her after the service and she was happy to chat with them.

Now sadly she must leave for London tomorrow and I will miss her so very much.   Alice will stay here with me.   She has taught Bridie all that she needs to know to take over as Bella's dresser, and is content for us to spend our retirement together.   Alice has helped Bella so much and she and I have had such busy lives.   I retired from the Dower House and it will be just grand to have my dear sister with me again.

Chapter 21   Bridie   1903

So here I am dresser and companion to one of the most famous singers in the world. It must be the luck of the Irish! Fancy I'll be seeing the world, or at least the inside of a lot of the world's concert halls.

Miss Arabella has changed since she came back from her Mum's. Maybe she misses her and Alice who she relied on for advice as well as company. I bet I'll be just as good. I know that I chatter a bit too much, but I've learned to keep quiet for the last twenty minutes before she's 'ON' and I'm brilliant at keeping the fans at bay.

We've had quite a long break. It's been lessons for her every day and sewing for me. She's decided to go into opera 'cos she can act as well as sing. I'll find it deadly boring waiting in the wings. On top of that she's told her agent to book her into recitals too. She's always had a lot of invites to private houses in America. Them rich folk like to boast that they've had someone as important as 'Arabella' to sing at their parties. I know she's told her agent to accept 'em if the fee is big enough!

Now we don't always get time to go to church for Miss Arabella and mass for me on Sundays. Instead we'll be off for lunch and a recital. Then it's early bed before we catch a train to her next engagement.

Somehow she still finds time to visit the great art galleries wherever we are. I don't see the point of staring at paintings, but it seems to make her happy.

Hugh Davenport was a great impresario. He had discovered Arabella, arranged her schedule as she learned her 'trade', and when she was ready had launched her career. His shrewd promotion together with her extraordinary talent had ensured her immediate success.

Thankfully she had been touring in Europe when Queen Victoria had died so she had not experienced any disruption to her schedules. Britain and the Empire mourned their Queen Empress. Hugh had hoped to present his young protégé to sing at court. Now he must wait for the new King to be crowned, and settled into his role. Edward's notorious eye for the ladies should ensure that Arabella would receive and enthusiastic reception. Her standing and fees would be even higher.

Arabella had undertaken all that he had asked of her, working hard to expand her repertoire, and enrich her voice ever further. Yet now he was receiving worrying reports from the agent he had appointed for her.   Alfred Millard was experienced, trustworthy and knew how to manage and encourage new talent.

Arabella's French and Italian were now good enough for her to move into light opera, where Puccini must come first. After her successful Paris debut she wanted to return to America as soon as possible with more performances and remunerative private engagements booked.

Arabella was also insisting that more of the postcards, which featured her in her many splendid costumes or pretty day clothes, must be sold.

She had requested a regular 'balance sheet' to show her income
and expenses. She must retain and pay for Fitz as her
accompanist and now needed a part time secretary to answer her
mail as well as Bridie and a maid at the hotels.

Already highly paid, Arabella was a valued source of income to
Hugh and his agent. He could not allow her to be 'priced out'.

Why had she become so money conscious? He quickly insisted
that she must appear in Vienna and Venice before he would allow
a return to America. Also Saltzburg to really get a feel for the
Strauss music which he intended to promote vigorously.

Arabella had at last returned to America.   After the rather safe
and stolid European tour, which Hugh Davenport had insisted
upon, it was a relief to return to the sheer vitality, enthusiasm and
get-up-and-go of America.

Hugh had been right of course and her command of the great
operatic scores had been re-assuring.   There were still many roles
that she was too young to tackle.   Some of Verdi and the whole of
Wagner, for she never could abide German.

Her European audiences had been respectful rather than wildly
enthusiastic, but they had heard the greatest Divas in the world.
By comparison, the Americans went wild for her.   City after city
saw standing ovations to gladden her heart.   Despite her English
rose colouring, her greatest role was to be Madame Butterfly!
This was made possible by clever wigs and makeup.   Hugh had
also ensured that she took classes in Japanese dance so that her
movements and gestures were accurate.   Of course her
audiences loved an American hero even if he did turn out to be a
heel!

Her Manon was willful and abandoned as befits a courtesan and
she received many hopeful gifts from male admirers.   Since these
were not only bouquets of flowers but a diamond bracelet or
necklet she gratefully accepted their tributes.

How could Arabella have guessed that her life was to completely
change on a balmy Sunday in the fall of 1906?

Arabella was collected from her hotel by the chauffeur driving a car of the family who had booked her and driven to the far outskirts of Boston. She knew of the Grantley family and of its enormous wealth. The family were involved in all kinds of philanthropy, were willing to pay an extraordinarily generous fee, and had one of the greatest art collections in America.

Their fortune had been hewn from their coalmines, tempered in their steel mills and forged from their railroads. Both rich and cultivated, she much anticipated her arrival at their fabulous estate. The car turned in between massive pillars, and seemed to drive for miles before the huge mansion came into view. It made Courtneys look like a country cottage.

Arabella was ushered in by a courtly butler to the hall where her hosts greeted her most warmly. It was rather like a receiving line, for she met the two daughters and their husbands, assorted aunts and uncles, together with several friends and neighbours.

Arabella was asked if she was ready for luncheon, but first had one special request.
'May I first please visit your gallery as I know that you collect British portraiture?"
'But of course' came the genial reply. 'Our son will conduct your there.'

The man who entered the room was slim and handsome, and she guessed, in his early thirties. It was only when he was introduced as Francis that she remembered the American tutor who had so improved her sketching at Courtneys. They smiled with mutual recognition, and excusing themselves, moved off to the renowned

59

gallery, which would one day be bequeathed to a grateful nation.

Along the great portraits they moved. Many were full length so that Arabella was able to admire the wonderful clothes and intricate detail. All the great names in British painting were represented. They both admired Gainsborough over Sir Joshua Reynolds. Kneller and Lely were a little repetitive, though did capture the luscious beauties of King Charles II's court.

Half way along, there hung a small painting by a hand, which she did not recognize. It was a pastel of a young girl wearing a pretty summer dress. Pink ribbons decorated her blond curls. One hand was outstretched as if to pluck a rose in a splendid rose garden. Her head was slightly lowered as if to savour its perfume.

Overcome she turned to Francis and asked, 'This is me isn't it, where were you?'
'Oh, in the little summerhouse, I sketched you quickly and painted it in a little later. It deserves its place here because of the delicacy and beauty of its subject.'

There was no time to continue the conversation as lunch was announced. This was light and delicious, but Arabella ate only sparingly and sipped only water.

She was to sing what she called here 'Afternoon Programme', after a short break. Fitz had joined them after lunch. Confident in her accompanist – which was not always the case on such occasions – she sang both lively and soulful songs and finished with an old English folk song 'Greensleeves'.

Her hostess rose to thank her in such a sincere and courtly style that she was reminded of Sir Edward, and felt unusually moved.

Among the guests was a tall still distinguished man with silver curly hair. He
looked somehow familiar and yet she knew that she had never met him before. He was introduced as Uncle Sean and his wife as Aunty Penelope. The man bent to kiss her hand in tribute to her performance. It was only then that she recognised him – for she saw his face in her mirror every day.

Arabella quickly stifled her exclamation, of shock and dismay. How could the man 'lost at sea' and lost to his child for so long be standing before her? She trembled slightly but her stage training stood her in good stead and she did not break down in the face of this huge shock.

Francis told her that Sean O'Donnell was an accomplished artist himself, but had established a reputable gallery in Boston. He imported and dealt in mainly Irish portraits and sporting pictures. Aunt Penelope had met him at the gallery, formed a valued connection and eventually married him.

'When was that?' she enquired innocently. 'They look so well matched'.
'Oh, quite recently in 1903 I think.   They are incredibly well suited and happy. He lives here now as part of the family and curates the collection'.

Arabella thought that her mother would find the conversation incredibly interesting!

Sean managed to extricate her from the guests on the pretext of showing her a portrait of special interest.

His admission was immediate.
'Yes I am your father, Arabella, and proud I am of you too. I hope that you can find it in your heart to forgive me for deserting you and your mother. I was far too young to be tied down with my whole future ahead of me, so I sailed to America'.

She saw the roguish twinkle in his eyes and felt the full blast of his irresistable Irish charm. NO wonder that her mother and so many other women, had found him too easy to succumb to.

Ostensibly discussing the picture, she made it clear that his secret was safe with her. Why disrupt such a happy 'marriage' and lifestyle? After all 50% of her genes were his. Still shaken to her core but apparently controlled she took her leave.

Thus she discovered her 'Lost at Sea' father and rediscovered Francis who she knew that she would marry one day.

By 1907 Arabella felt confident in her finances. It would have
been so easy to accept Francis's oft repeated proposal of
marriage. She always gave him the same answer 'Of course – but
not yet. I have something that I must do'.

Two letters reached her in Philadelphia causing the only
cancellation of a performance that she ever made in her entire
career. The first was from the Estate Manager at Courtneys
laying out the disastrous situation there. The second was from
her London solicitors. At thirty-one Richard had been forced to
admit defeat. He was now so deeply mired in debt that his
creditors – so many of them – refused to wait any longer for the
promised return of their money. For the first time in two
hundred years Courtneys was to be sold.

The trustees agreed that should a credible buyer appear they
might allow the estate to accompany it, but the money from that
estate must stay in trust until Richard was thirty-five. He could
only look to the house sale and Courtneys was now so shabby and
depleted is value must be depressed.

Only two slovenly maids remained, with one groom and old Finch
struggling with the help of a boy to maintain the kitchen garden.
The cook kept going on whatever drink she could lay her hands
on.

Her lawyer's letter informed Arabella that, in line with her
instructions, they had made an anonymous offer a little above the
asking price. They had confirmed to the trustees that if the offer

was successful on the house their client would be in a position to enter into negotiations for the estate when Richard reached thirty-five.

Richard did not wait to hear the result of the trustees' deliberations. He took the offer, transferred the money, paid off the most threatening of his creditors, stalled the others, and smartly disappeared.

Before leaving Philadelphia Bella completed her last few concerts, bade adieu to her entourage and sailed for England, keen to see once again her much loved Courtneys, but when Arabella arrived to take over her home she found it empty and unlocked. She leaned her forehead and palms of her hands against the warm golden stone. She felt again all the love from her days as the maid who had lavished such care on Courtneys. Its warmth caressed her back.

Touring the house from attics to cellars was a sobering experience. She wrote on the pad that she carried to record the most urgent work to be done just a single word –

-EVERYTHING-

Well ah've bin me own boss for years now.   Master Richard fergits to pay me any wages.   Ah've just pottered round in the vegetable garden, takin me time and doin what ah could wi' little 'elp. Ah've had to let Lady Cynthisa's rose garden go to pot.

She'll be right upset if she ever comes back to Courtneys – not that ah thinks as she will wi' Mr. Richard's wild drunken friends. Them maids are no better'n they should be.   Still yer can't blame 'em for makin an extra bob or two on the side.   Now they've all run off an 'ere I am.   Master of all ah surveys.

Spoke too soon! But then it 'appended – There ah was singin one o' me songs an' loud an' clear the gret voice joins in.   Well if it weren't that little minx Arabella.   So ah gets me duet at last.   It were grand!

She tells me its her wot's bought the house and she'll be movin' in wi' two new maids an her little Irish lass.   Ah'l get a new lad to 'elp me out.

She tells me as 'ow me vegetable garden looks good.   O' course she then went and spoiled it.

'Oh Mr. Finch, I do so hope we can get the roses back in order. It'll need a lot of manure'.

DANG AND BLAST IT!

The house seemed to know that Arabella was back.

Donning my wrapper and headscarf I set to the next morning to give the kitchen range a proper clean. It lit at once as Finch had made sure that there was plenty of kindling.

By the time Bridie and the two maids arrived there were kettles of hot water ready and my mother had provided plenty of clean cloths, soap, brushes, polishes and anything else we would need.

I had already swept out, scrubbed down the kitchen table and dusted the chairs. We sat down for a cup of hot tea and a council of war.

Finch was early with his box of vegetables, fruits and salads. He nodded to the maids, took a mug of tea and ambled off singing to himself.

The girls had been engaged by my mother. 'Sturdy sensible girls'. 'They'll work till they drop for you' she said. 'They're that glad that Courtneys will be in good hands, and it doesn't hurt that you're famous. They'll be the envy of all their friends.'

I suggested that Bridie take over the kitchen while Edie and Millie needed to make three bedrooms fit for use. One each for Bridie and me and one for the girls to share. We identified them, stripped them down to basics, cleaned them as only good maids can, and waited for my mother and Alice to arrive with clean bedding. We were all on the first floor, which surprised Edie and

Millie. We would be closer together and far fewer steps to climb.

After a quick breakfast, of course I tackled the library where I cleared out all

Richard's rubbish and set up my office. After Bridie's quick soup and egg salad lunch we just carried on. The girls preferred to work straight through, have supper and then be finished for the day.

My Mother and Alice arrived with more groceries and clean bedding. Then we all trooped up to the servants' quarters. Under my Mother's direction we threw the rubbish out of the windows for Finch's giant bonfire. He was like a child on November 5th.   Mother labeled which furniture was to go, while Alice made a list of essential replacements.

As Mrs. Seymour, my mother had always kept journals which listed everything – the dates when the chimneys were swept, when curtains were renewed, when Spring cleaning started – dependent on when the family were away, how long this great upheaval took and details of the household linen and laundry. Also what supplies she bought and her household accounts, plus the names of the staff as they came and left. Birthdays and deaths – all were recorded and I determined to carry on the practice. I certainly had plenty of empty shelves on which to store them.

Each afternoon I retired to the Library and practiced my scales and voice exercises. This was essential so that I could accept any engagement at short notice. The purchase of the house had left my funds low, and I was determined to pay the staff wages on time.

The Trustees had agreed to operate the estate until Richard was thirty-five as decided at their appointment. Then I must then agree to buy or withdraw.

I had assured Bridie and the girls that I would not make extra work and expense by constantly entertaining. When I did so we would offer tea, coffee and hot chocolate with some of my Mother's fancy biscuits, Bridie's special

Irish fruit cake, which seemed to feature quite a lot of Irish whiskey and proved to be very popular. They were meant to take it in turns to cook supper but my lively Irish dresser proved her worth by having nourishing soups, omelettes, stews and fruit and vegetables from the garden ready in a flash.

Before we started on the ground floor rooms the builders arrived. They and the heating engineer were to be my main expense, and saw the secret sale of my jewelry gifts.

Living in splendid American hotels had given me a taste for central heating. Its installation would cause major disruption; but the expert had assured me that feeding the pipes under the floorboards and fixing brass grills to allow the warm air into the rooms would be quite easy. Their carpenters would follow making good, then plasterers if needed followed by the decorators. It all sounded very efficient and hugely expensive, even before it all connected to a new boiler! To make matters worse what bathrooms there were, were primitive and horrible.

I unrealistically wished to provide bathrooms at the end of both the female and male staff corridors and also wished there to be a kitchen – only small – for each corridor.   Then I wanted some dividing walls demolished so that each room could house a small sitting area.

I was determined that Bridie and the maids would not be waiting on workmen all day.   Harsh though it seems they were to live in the rooms over the stables and carriage sheds and cater for themselves.   Or they could go home at the end of each day to lodgings in the village.   This some of them chose to do and several romances developed as a result.

I had seriously underestimated the cost of these major changes, which were proving huge and we had not even addressed the provision of one bathroom between two bedrooms for the family and guest bedrooms.

This meant that I must immediately take on a London season, which Hugh was able to arrange for me at short notice.

Mother and Alice were to move in to help, and the estate agent had kindly agreed to look in too.

It was a relief to escape all the turmoil and to renew my links with London and its theatrical music and art scene.   I had not perhaps realised how draining all the work was proving, without worrying about the expense.   The costumes from my American tour were unseen in England and Bridie refurbished them with style.   Hugh was at his splendid helpful best.   The newspapers had featured my purchase of Courtneys.   The headlines carried between 'Opera Star Buys Country Estate' to 'FORMER UNDER MAID BUYS

THE HOUSE WHERE SHE CLEANED'. In any event both sold newspapers and tickets, which pleased Hugh mightily.

I owed so much to Hugh. His guidance and decisions were always so helpful to me. He had given his blessing to my purchase of the house and understood my need for the money to do so. He knew that my overriding love for my music and the wonderful career and fame, which it had brought me would bind me to him.

There were mixed results when I returned home with Bridie four weeks later. Our hard work at Courtneys followed by demanding rehearsals and performances had taken their toll. It had been brilliant to work with Fitz again and I dined with Hugh Davenport to discuss plans for future promotions.

The staff floor, which I preferred to servants, was now almost finished. I had chosen fresh white walls with pale green or lemon doors for the female corridor. Different shades of blue were used for the men's corridor doors though when we would be able to afford male staff was open to debate.

Alice had made new curtains and bedspreads in matching check or stripes and the results were fresh and pleasing. With the new bathrooms and cheery crockery in the two small kitchens all was snug.

On the main bedroom floor there were problems. The installation of six new bathrooms was over- ambitious. The water pressure was weak and supply was inadequate.

Too weary to worry, I retired to the Library were Bridie brought me a tray of tea and toast, and left me to open my letters. As I was reading one from Francis, a shadow fell across my desk. Looking up, I saw Christopher Richards standing inside the open French windows.

We shook hands firmly in the American way. Christopher took tea and whiskey cake and then came to the reason for his call. To be neighbourly of course, and to welcome me personally. Almost shyly he confessed that he had never forgotten me singing at his 21st birthday party. Would I perhaps care to go for a drive with him for he knew that I refused to ride? He would book lunch at a very respectable hotel for us. Or perhaps a game of tennis, with afternoon tea? I gazed at this earnest young man in puzzlement. Did he not realize that I had never played tennis in my life?

About to refuse I suddenly decided that a total break might be very welcome. So began a friendship, which gave us both much pleasure. Christopher would ride or motor over from Rossiters for he was an early motor enthusiast.

We would walk in the woods for he was a naturalist too, or just sit in the still neglected rose garden with coffee or tea. Aware of my many responsibilities he allowed me to tell him when I would be available to set out for a drive.

The continuing disruption and inability to resolve the bathroom problems began to affect household morale. What had begun as a great adventure was becoming hugely expensive and burdensome. At least the heating system was working though the new boiler seemed to eat fuel.
It was Bridie who saved us with her ready Irish wit and vibrant

nature. She could always be relied upon to cheer us all up with a joke or an Irish jig. I usually took my coffee in the library but today Bridie asked if we could all meet.

'Them builders are getting us all down. I reckon that they are taking advantage of Miss Arabella. What say you make them clear up and push off for now. The heating is working, we can have fires in the dining room and drawing room, decorate up for Christmas and have a grand evening with mulled wine and mince pies. If they drink enough and Miss Arabella sings it'll be great. We can finish with carols too.'

'If Miss Arabella can manage without me for her next series of London concerts, we can push on here'.

We walked through the hall and agreed that if we 'shine up' the two other major rooms and 'Decked the hall with boughs of holly' and mistletoe and greenery, it would hide many of the gaps left by missing furniture and pictures.

Bridie seemed to have several gentlemen friends who could help with the heavy work for the pleasure of her laughing Irish eyes.

I felt we could manage to afford a daily cook who would come in each morning, cook the lunch and prepare a warming evening meal for Bridie to complete and serve. This would leave Bridie free to work with Edie and Millie preparing the reception rooms and ladies cloakroom. I had not told even Bridie that I had needed to ask Hugh for a large advance on my future salary. Without an estate to bring in rents and income I had seriously underestimated how costly my plans for Courtneys would be.

I set off for the London train with my trunk packed by Bridie and my scores ready. I had sent out my invitations, which clearly stated that the party was to take place between 8pm and 11pm. I felt lighter of heart and more optimistic for the future. I had hoped that the work at Courtneys would have been nearer completion. I had perhaps been over-ambitious, but wanted only the best for my wonderful house.

I trusted the three girls, their helpers and Mother and Alice who were to undertake all the flower and greenery arrangements. Even Finch was not immune to Bridie who always teased him when he collected his tea and Irish cake. I sometimes caught them singing together. He called Bridie a 'saucy maid', as he had once called me. I was now 'Miss Arablella' and to be respected for finding him a new boy to help in the garden and for re-instating his wages.

My hotel was booked and a maid waited to unpack my small trunk. My performance trunk would go with me to the Royal Albert Hall, where a dresser had been engaged.

I always loved this week. The programme consisted of the sacred music I had grown up with, and which I found so much less demanding than recital or operatic music.

I freely admitted to myself that my breaks with Christopher had enlivened yet relaxed me, after the interminable demands and worries of my first months at Courtneys. What had begun with high expectations had curdled into a morass of problems. Perhaps Bridie was right, and the builders were taking advantage.

The week of nightly concerts went well. My voice was rested full and still a wonderful instrument for me. The evening always finished with the audience joining in with the beloved carols. 'Oh Come All Ye Faithful' concluded the event. The concertgoers sang it with such fervour and we encored it together. To cries of 'Happy Christmas', I left the stage happy and elated.

I always expect dignitaries and well-wishers to visit my dressing room after any performance. Bridie knew not to attempt to relieve me of my finale costume until the last one had left.

As I entered, a well known and beloved voice said 'Hello darling, well done, you were wonderful.'

I was at once enfolded in Francis's arms. Our reunion was extra special because it was so unexpected. Our kisses were at first fierce with longing and then tender with love.

A gentle knocking reminded me that I had other people waiting. Then in they came, all wanting a word, a smile and to see me at close quarters. I did not feel so exposed if I was still wearing my stage costume and make up. At last they left and I was able to change and drive with Francis to my hotel for a quiet supper. We didn't even begin to catch up before I needed to get to bed. How I longed to ask him to join me! He might have been surprised, but I saw from the desire in his eyes that he could not have resisted.

Too many watching eyes willing to sell stories to newspapers. My reputation won over desire, but he would call to escort me to breakfast – no doubt with champagne, so I would need to look my best. Luckily I had a divine dress and jacket by Patou, which he had not seen. I knew that colour just highlighted my colouring and its cut enhanced my hourglass figure.

Since King Edward had succeeded to the throne after his dour mother, London and its social like had sprung into action. Here were women of the greatest beauty who were unafraid to flaunt the wealth of their admirers, and who attracted much interest. Their likenesses were on postcards everywhere, and I had even seen Lily Langtry.

Francis and I spent as much time together as my schedule would allow. He insisted on taking me to Bond Street to choose my engagement ring. It will remain a secret until we announce it at the Courtneys Christmas Party.

All was activity and bustle when Arabella and Francis arrived at Courtneys. He remembered the house in its heyday with Sir Charles and Lady Cynthia, and the three children enjoying his classes. It really was a shadow of its former self, and yet he recognised that its basic beauty and structure was intact.

When Francis had been introduced to Bridie, Bella led him on a tour of her home. He at once saw that she had ordered too much work at once. Until the bathroom and water problems were resolved she could not move on. So he formulated a plan.

They observed that the great staircase was polished and its carpet was cleaned. The black and white tiles in the great hall gleamed, Arabella saw to her astonishment that the empty wall spaces were now covered by several splendid tapestries. Though slightly faded, they added grandeur to the hall more pleasing than the previous portraits. Bridie had raided the old storerooms. Her finds extended to less worthy paintings, some interesting pieces of furniture and sets of crockery, which had been packed away when new ones were purchased.

Helped by Evelyn's recollections and journals they had unearthed some gems, which had evaded Richard. These once again graced the main rooms, but it was the standard of the cleaning so that everything shone and glittered which so impressed her. Shabby chairs and settees looked less so – just comfortable with freshly washed covers and new cushion covers. The mirrors gleamed and everywhere were great masses of greenery.   Plinths stood ready awaiting her Mother's arrangements. Candles and lamps were in place. They may have been an assortment, but once lit and with Fitz invited to play as guests arrived it would work well. Arabella could not wait to rush to the kitchen to thank them all for their outstanding and inventive work.

The acceptances poured in from neighbours, tenants, helpers, choristers, clergy – in fact so many who had been such a part of Courtneys life. Finch told his boy to smarten up and be ready to keep the fires going, to add cheerfulness.

Two of Bridie's Irishmen (in the footmen's clothes) were to serve the punch. The maids were to hand round the mince pies, Irish whiskey cake and whatever sweetmeats the cook and Evelyn could produce. Another handsome Irishman was to take the ladies' cloaks and the gentlemen's hats and coats. The boy had to be ready to wash up the glasses, so casually discarded, when the maids collected them. Bridie had warned that they had too few and had borrowed a large number from Mrs. Richards, crossing her fingers that none would be broken.

Christmas Eve arrived all too soon. Francis had insisted on installing a large Christmas tree and decorating it. With the candles and lamps lit, fires blazing and Fitz playing lively Music Hall tunes, all was ready.

Flaming torches lined the approach to the house. Everyone arrived dressed in their best and in high good humour.

Arabella was never quite sure how the evening became such a success. Even those few who had arrived ready to criticize, for there was now no Courtney at the house after more than two centuries, were in good heart. The usual class distinctions seemed not to matter.   The ladies mixed, whispered and giggled over the punch.   The gentlemen were soon discussing the weather, the Boxing Day hunt, the shoots, their gardens and the new fangled automobiles.   Their complexions grew rather flushed.

Soon Francis, who Arabella seemed to have introduced to dozens of people, called the company to order.   There were far too many guests for them all to
be seated, so the ladies took the chairs while the gentlemen stood at the back.
Arabella stepped onto the dais.   At once she launched into all the old favourite songs, which everyone could enjoy.

Of course in the end it was Archie Finch who was the star turn. He and Bridie had turned out one of the old dress suits perhaps from COLLINGS the old head butler before RANSOME. He had rehearsed with Bridie and given Fitz the music from his song score. As soon as Arabella stepped down for a break Fitz played a 'drum roll' and up stepped Finch.

The audience was astonished. It had been 'Bad form' when Cynthia Courtney had allowed her maid to sing at Sir Charles's birthday, and now the gardener was about to repeat the 'faux pas'! Looking at handsome Irish footmen, some of the ladies wondered what other talents might be laying hidden at Courtneys!

Finch was not to be deterred. He sang lustily and surprisingly tunefully for an old man. The applause was generous and sincere. He'd showed 'em. His mates at the pub couldn't pull 'is leg now when 'e was a bit worse for wear and gave 'em a tune. He could die happy now.

Arabella returned, and they all joined together with songs and carols. All too soon it was 10.30p.m.   Tots of whiskey were served to the gentlemen, and more punch for the ladies saw glasses filled.

Calling for attention once silence ensued Francis made their engagement announcement. To applause and shouts of congratulations, they kissed and he placed the magnificent ring on her finger. Arabella caught Christopher looking at her with longing. They had been good companions and he had helped her through a difficult summer, but she had never given him any hint of romantic interest. She smiled and waved to him.

Then it was time for everyone to don their coats and hats and walk down to St. Bart's for Midnight Service.

Bridie appeared flushed and happy at the success of their first party. Suddenly Arabella knew the secret of that success. The constant press of people round the mulled wine table was the give away. Her own glass had been particularly delicious. Of course! The Irishmen had laced it with either whiskey or brandy. The warm mince pies were plump with brandy-laced mincemeat, and the whiskey cake was more redolent than ever with Irish whiskey. She hoped that they all sobered up before they arrived in church. She was content to sit at the back with Francis, holding hands and just humming the well loved carols.

The choir were in full voice, the sermon brief, the Merry Christmases sincere and she had her fiancé at her side. She kissed her mother and Alice fondly as they separated until Christmas lunch.

Walking back, soft flakes of snow began to fall. With the maids chattering behind them they greeted Christmas day 1907 with hope and joy in their hearts.

Cook, Finch and a tired young lad had cleared away the party debris and gone home with cook well rewarded, and Alfie amazed to see that Francis had slipped him a golden sovereign. Whatever would his Ma say?

As the maids and Bridie went up to bed Arabella led Francis into the Library, stoked up the fire and then very deliberately seduced him. Now that they were officially committed she felt no embarrassment as she removed her dress displaying her lavish body to him.

Nature took its course as nature will. Being a gentleman he did wonder at her confidence but decided to put such thoughts aside, and enjoy the lushness of his love.

Arabella wondered in her turn finding Francis self-assured, at first fiery and then tender. It was a meeting of minds as well as bodies. They realised that in their coupling there was compatability and the promise of a full and happy union. Quietly they ascended the great staircase and moved to her bedroom. At least the w/c flushed in the bathroom.

Bella awoke to a bright crisp Christmas morning with lying snow, and a wonderland of trees and bushes covered in fairy tale frost. Francis had gone, for, mindful of her reputation, he had slipped quietly away after they had made love again in the comfort of her bed. Bella stretched luxuriantly looking around her room, which was shabby but comfortable. She knew at once how she would express her love for Courtneys.

Donning her working clothes she descended the staircase savouring every step. With her hand on the polished banister she felt the history and essence of her beloved house. All her struggles to rescue it seemed as nothing in the face of its history and the generation of Courtneys who had lived there. Now they had given way to a former housemaid.
Truly ARABELLA AUGUSTA LOUISA SEYMOUR was at home.

So it was that she was back in time, to when she lit and nursed the fires and cleaned the grates. Bella started the kitchen range so that when Bridie, Edie, Millie and Cook arrived all was ready for a quick breakfast and a gossip about last night's party. What fun and what a delightful success it had been.

Soon they were all working to provide a fine Christmas lunch. After much discussion it had been agreed that this would be taken in the kitchen. It was warmer and more friendly than the formal dining room and it meant that the food would not cool being carried through. Also Arabella firmly believed that they had worked together so hard then so they should enjoy Christmas together.

Francis had made good use of his time in London for there arrived two large hampers.   Exotic fruits which Finch could no longer produce in the abandoned tropical greenhouse, candied fruit, chocolates, all manner of exotic sweetmeats, cheeses and of course a great turkey and cuts of beef which delighted cook and set the gastric juices flowing in anticipation   A smaller hamper warned DO NOT OPEN and was set aside awaiting Francis's arrival.

When Arabella asked Bridie , who was stoking the boiler, that lady replied with a cheeky smile, and a finger to the side of her nose to say 'Don't ask Miss Arabella'.

Thus warned, Arabella took her coffee to the Library.   She still had much correspondence to open but just sat quietly absorbing the ravaged bookshelves and feeling somehow, somewhere the spirit of dear Sir Edward.   She imagined his distress and determined that she would return it to life with its shelves polished and refurbished.   And she regretted the loss of the great Audubon Book of American Birds.   Wretched, wretched Richard.

Bella rose to go upstairs and change into a suitable but simple outfit of plum velvet skirt, ruffled blouse and wide belt to accentuate her wasp waist.

She saw the single golden rose, which Finch had somehow saved from the frost and left for her. So he had got a heart, and had surprised and delighted her guests too.

Christmas lunch was to be served at 2p.m.   Arabella was surprised to see the long table set for twelve people.   The white tablecloth sparkled and down its centre was a garland of greenery.   Set along it were glass stands – for the silver epergnes were long gone – of peaches, pineapples, pears and cascades of luscious black and white grapes. Shiny red applies were dotted among the foliage and there was a centerpiece of red flowers.

Francis arrived having collected her Mother and Aunt Alice. Kisses and Christmas greetings were exchanged, and she noticed that there were bottles of champagne cooling and wines and ales on the dresser. Her curiosity was aroused and soon satisfied as first Finch, still sporting his finery of last night arrived. He was closely followed by the cheerful sound of manly Irish voices preceding the three 'Irish boys' who had so ably helped at the party and ensured its success. It was a happy and lively scene.

Francis handed out glasses of champagne. The table was admired by Evelyn, who saw in Bridie a worthy success as Housekeeper and determined to gift her all her journals of Courtneys.

Soon the table groaned with the fine turkey, beef and all the vegetables and sauces, which make the Christmas meal such a feast. Liam and Paddy carved. The pudding was set alight to many Oh's and Ah's and thoroughly enjoyed in all its glory. Only the men had room for the cheeses while the ladies contented themselves with a little fruit.

Toasts were proposed by Francis especially to 'Cook – 'the founder of the feast'. Ethel could hardly believe it. Here she sat at table with the Mistress and Mr. Francis, and they were toasting her! When Francis resumed his seat, Archibald Finch rose ponderously to his feet. His announcement surprised Arabella. He swore to them all that having failed to graft a rose for Lady

Cynthia or himself he was determined to put aside his dislike of the rose garden and to produce a 'Miss Arabella' rose. He thanked them all for the best company and Christmas dinner, he had ever shared. After the 'Hear, Hear's' had died away he proposed a heartfelt toast –

'To Miss Arabella – the saviour of Courtneys'

Arabella blushed prettily as Francis opened the magic hamper and handed out the gifts. Blue wrapping paper for the men and pink with gold ribbon for the ladies. All were well chosen and as Bridie had warned her before hand, the Irish contingent had not been forgotten.

Bella gently asked her Mother to accompany her to the library. Evelyn was by now almost seventy and had aged since her retirement. They shared a fond embrace and Bella poured out her love and gratitude to the woman who had given her so much. First her grand name then all the love and encouragement to live up to it, so that she had grown up unafraid of hard work and with the determination to succeed.

Evelyn looked at her 'Golden Girl' and saw a woman of substance of whom she was inordinately proud. World famous perhaps, but still with the background and grit which had given her the strength not only to succeed, but to work so hard to buy Courtneys, rescue Courtneys where Evelyn had spent over fifty years of her own life from the clutches of the wretched Richard. Surely happier days lay ahead. Returning to the company the party took coffee and brandy. Then the Irishmen, including the mystery stoker departed taking Finch with them. Bridie, Edie,

Millie and cook cleared up and chatted over cups of tea, while Francis drove Evelyn and Alice home tired but happy.   It had been a Christmas to remember.

So it proved as Francis and Arabella plotted the year ahead. She had many engagements to fulfill and did not wish to default on any of them. Although concerned with her schedule, Francis told her of his plan for Courtneys. He wanted to draft in Mike Roberts to oversee all the remaining building work.

Mike Roberts was a trusted and experienced man who would stand no malingering or excuses. He intended to employ only capable and experienced workers and to oversee them closely. He was only thirty-five but was a valued employee of the Grantley family and would see the work completed not only swiftly, but to the standards which the house deserved.

'He sounds splendid', said Arabella, 'but how can I possibly afford him as well as the builders'? 'Quite easily my dear girl' her fiancé replied. 'It will be my wedding gift to you. I also propose that you make Bridie not only Housekeeper but House Manager. Her salary will need to be increased, but she will not be subject to the authority of any man. She has a charming way with her, and should she employ any future male staff, they need not include a butler. She already manages the Irish boys well and has you, your Mother and Alice to refer to. I know that you can rely on her utterly as you did when she was your dresser and companion. I also propose that you keep on Paddy as general handyman and for security reasons. He can patrol around the house and help the maids with heavy work too. Mickie can look after the two horses and help Finch while Liam can return to his job as a builder. They can stay in the rooms over the stables. Roberts will ensure that they all know the workings of the boiler thoroughly'.

Arabella saw that he had thought his plan through and saw no
reason to disagree with any part of it. Her optimism and hopes
for Courtneys seemed more achievable now with lovely Francis by
her side.

'Francis, my darling, I have something I want to put to you. When
I was so exhausted last summer I asked by agent to arrange my
engagements so as to allow a month's summer break. I had
intended to spend it here, but now feel that I would like to go to
Switzerland. The air will be good for my lungs and voice and I am
less likely to have people always staring at me. Do you think that
you could return from America to join me?'

'Darling girl of course! I'll be back working with Pa and the
brothers-in-law straight after the New Year, so they won't object'.
Arabella smiled and said 'Do you think also that we might get
married and use it as our honeymoon?'
At first Francis thought that he had misheard. Her huge violet
eyes were so expressive that he could not mistake their message.
Sweeping her into his arms and pressing longing kisses on her
delicious mouth he left her in no doubt as to his reply.

I may be a fiery red-headed Irish girl but I know how to keep a secret. Before I came to work for Miss Arabella I'd dressed ladies who reputations would have been shattered if I'd opened my mouth to the newspapers. And I'd have been quids in.

When I was asked to meet her in the library and to bring my notepad and her Ma's journal for the year of Sir Charles's marriage to Lady Cynthia the penny still didn't drop! My jaw must have dropped a foot when she told me about her wedding plans.

So here's this little Irish girl, holding even more and more secrets and party to all kinds of subterfuge. Miss Arabella had worked out the number of guests and would send out last minute invitations. Obviously the vicar would need to know and folk would find out about it when the banns were read. The choir would need to be in good voice too as Miss Bella did not intend to sing at her own wedding!

Here I was with a list as long as me arm and all to be accomplished at the last minute! Good thing that I know how to work miracles – that is with Mr Francis's money behind me. With that I can move mountains.

Paddy is a great help with so much heavy work and this American Mike Roberts will soon whip the new builders into shape. I am looking forward to meeting him.

Then she got me with a final knockout blow.   I'm to be House

Manager! Me jaw dropped again and I couldn't help but give Miss Arabella a big hug.

LET'S GET TO IT I SAY WE'LL MAKE COURTNEYS SOMETHING WONDERFUL BY JUNE

When Arabella left for her tour of America she did so with a new repertoire and new costumes.   Hugh Davenport and her agent ensured that all arrangements were as well organized as usual. This was to be a series of recitals, with quite serious music.   The American audiences were mad for culture feeling that their patronage to such a programme reflected on their own sophistication.   Advance ticket sales were more than promising, so all augured well.

A visit to Patou in Paris en route had replenished her personal wardrobe with the latest styles, which would impress in America.

One particular gown was to go to Courtneys in early June marked for the especial attention of Bridie only.

Accompanying Bella as dresser and companion was a double of Bridie. It was in fact her sister, Maire, who had been 'trained' up by Bridie.   What was it about the Irish which made them so cheerful and effective?   And what fun too?   Arabella found herself laughing so much with Maire.   She disarmed all the back stage crew, charmed the dressing room callers and made so many tips that Arabella teased her that she would soon be able to retire back to Ireland.

As they criss-crossed America Francis and Arabella were sometimes able to spend Saturday evening, Sunday and part of Monday together before they took separate journeys onwards. Bella tried to keep up with her old routine of visiting galleries and exhibitions.   The beauty of the exhibits refreshed her world and increased her knowledge. Without the splendid railways they could not have covered such huge distances in such comfort. The rolling stock was new and their compartments so comfortable that both slept well on overnight journeys. By dressing severely, pinning up her hair and not letting her English accent give her away, she and Maire were able to enjoy their meals mainly in peace.

Despite her success, Arabella was beginning to wonder if her recitals were becoming a little too staid and conservative, perhaps too predictable. America had such energy and vitality that Arabella felt that her performances needed to reflect this. Did she need to alter her image? She must discuss it with Hugh Davenport and be guided by his experience.

The busy weeks flew by like the places they saw from the train window.

The weather had been uncertain, and two performances were cancelled because of heavy snow but, snug and warm in their hotel, Arabella and Maire made the most of their unexpected time off. It was imperative that Bella protect her voice, so they took their meals in Bella's room so as to avoid people with coughs and colds. Thankfully the weather improved. Her voice was even more mature and mellifluous and the audiences as responsive and enthusiastic as ever, yet Bella felt that something within her was missing. Of course it was Courtneys and her Mother. Bridie's letters reassured her that Evelyn was holding her own. The English winter had been less severe than usual, and an early Spring gladdened their hearts. Evelyn seemed stronger and in good spirits too.   Alice remained a tower of strength and the solace of Sunday morning service at St Bart's was still to be cherished.

Francis reported that Roberts had indeed revitalised the building and plumbing work, having won the workers' respect for his knowledge skills and readiness to 'muck in'.

Francis and Bella's meetings were precious to them both, and their love was deepened by their frequent separations. He never tired of hearing her sing on Saturday evenings, often closing his eyes so that the glorious sounds bathed him in a kind of ecstasy. Now he waited for her dressing room to empty before taking her out to supper. They tended to avoid the great fashionable restaurants so that they could eat and talk in peace. When they did appear publicly they were always seated prominently, and all eyes were on them, which made Francis feel uncomfortable.

There always seemed to be photographers waiting for them too. The headline featured "The Golden Couple' and this is how they came to be known. Despite their overwhelming desire for each other Francis refused to be seen leaving her hotel. It was only during a week's break in April that he was able to spirit Bella away to an isolated cabin in woodland. The cabin had every possible aid to comfort and they spent their time either enjoying these comforts or in bed.

They had no staff and Bella's household skills soon returned. Her other skills were developing nicely when it was time for them to part and to go their separate ways again – he to his family's business and she to resume her concert tour. Arabella had never sung her 'Butterfly' aria 'One Fine Day' with such longing and pathos, nor her 'Manon Lescaux' with such abandon or received such wild applause and glowing reviews. If only they knew.

One late June morning Arabella's liner docked in Southampton.
Maire supervised the unloading of their luggage. Arabella
refused to stay in London, just changing stations and trains so as
to reach Courtneys by early evening. Calling at the cottage she
took her beloved mother in her arms, feeling how frail she had
become. Over Evelyn's shoulder she saw Alice quietly shake her
head. Of course she had splendid gifts for the two dearest ladies
in her life, but the greatest of all was to be together again. No
stylish clothes or fancy gifts could hide the huge love which
existed between them all. At last Arabella dragged herself away
and was driven to Courtneys.

An early dusk had fallen and yet the house blazed with light. Hearing her car approaching Bridie, Maire, Edie and Millie were waiting outside two either side of the door.   Arabella felt like falling to her knees and kissing the ground, but contented herself with her usual salute to Courtneys by leaning against the warm stone before entering.   At once she saw why the house had appeared to have dozens of candles flowing behind each window. In her absence Francis had ordered the installation of electricity in all rooms and a powerful generator.

The great English restorative of tea and toast must wait until she had toured all the downstairs rooms and marveled at the flood of light, which added such vitality at the touch of a switch.   Two huge chandeliers alight with dozens of bulbs hung in the great hall.   They illuminated the freshly decorated walls where only one tapestry remained.   On either side were the Courtney family portraits – not all of them – but enough to restore the feel of a great family house.

The small sitting room was now set out as her office with mountains of post on the desk.   Puzzled she saw a large 'DO NOT ENTER' on the door of the libray, only to find it locked.   Bridie looked particularly conspiratorial, but just shrugged her shoulders.
Sharing tea and toast in the kitchen, she thanked them all from the bottom of a full heart aware of all the upheaval they must have endured – all the dirt and dust and banging all day long. They would certainly deserve a bonus and a holiday after the wedding.

Well'ere we goes agin.   There's bin naut but 'ustle an' bustle and builders bangin' an' crashin'for months.   Naw this new fangled electrics is takin' over.   I may not 'old wi' it, but at least ah'l not ave to lug all that kindlin' for the fires, except on special occasions, so there's some good, in it.   An' I likes that young Mike Roberts, that American wot Mr Francis 'as sent over to knock them builders into shape an' keep 'em at the job – 'e's done wonders 'e 'as.

Some days e'll bring 'is tea into the garden an' sit wi' me for a while.   We 'as a chat an' puts the world to rights.   They'm getting' a bit windy in America 'cos the ruddy Germans are buildin' gret big 'Dreadnaught' ships.   Well them Germans 'ave allus wanted an empire like old Queen Victoria's.   They might be 'dreadnaught' now but once our lads get round 'em, they'll start dreadin.

We'm 'ad Nelson, so nobody on't sea can beat us nor land neither after Wellington saw off Napoleon at Waterloo.   I like me 'history an' Mike 'll sometimes drop into the pub for a pint.   Ah can tell by 'is face that 'e 'ates the taste, but enjoys the lads' company.

That Irish lad that lives over the stables keeps a look out round the 'ouse at night.
No body'd want to tangle wi' 'im an' that big cudgel 'e carries!

'Ere's some news.   I 'ated that rose garden once ah couldn't graft a rose for Lady Cynthia.   Ah'd never go in it agin, were she not always naggin' an' findin' me jobs.   Any road ah got a bit merry at

Christmas an' vowed to grow a rose for Miss Arabella. Too soon to tell yet but me an' the lad 'ave got the garden in good shape. Ah'm to 'ave a great honour at the weddin' that feisty maid Bridie tells me.

Don't tell me they want me to sing agin'! Ah'm still gettin' over the latest shock. Even wi' the extra 'elp o' Paddy ah've still not got on top o' the borders, an prunin' espalier fruit trees. It's a lot o' work an' bendin' an' ah'm not as young as ah used to be. Bridie wants everythin' tip top for the weddin' so ah'm to git a new gardener.

When 'e cum for me to interview 'im I finds 'im checkin' the cabbages for whitefly – cheeky devil! 'E looked to be wearn' good boots an' corduroy trousers an' a cap to keep the sun off. When 'e turned round, dang an ' blast it, if it weren't a woman! Ah were fair flabbergasted. She seemed quite respectful an' look strong wi' good big 'ands. Ah walked her round the borders askin' 'er questions as to 'ow she would improve 'em.

Why is it ah'm surrounded by wimmin at a time in me life when ah'm too owd to appreciate 'em?

This Maggie Jones was the only gardener – apart from meself – who knew all the botanical names o' the plants, as well as 'ow best to care for 'em. An' blow me if she didn't know most o' the roses an' all. Ah looks at the names in me journal every night when ah fills it in. That's so's ah remembers 'em an' be able to impress all them posh folks as 'll be comin' round once Miss Arabella's married and settled 'ere.

So Maggie got the job an' straight way whipped off 'er coat, put on 'er hessian apron an' got stuck into the borders. Now to tell 'er we've only got 12 days afore the weddin' to git all the beddin' plants in.

After breakfast, Mike Roberts arrived to show me all the alterations and improvements carried out in my absence. Notebooks at the ready, we started at the top.

The staff rooms were now fewer and larger. All the new curtains and bed linen had to be moved out for the walls to be knocked out and the electric cables to be installed. Replaced in the re-decorated rooms all looked welcoming. I was confident that, should we hold a house party in the future any visiting staff would be comfortable. Edie, Millie, Bridie and Maire assured me that they loved the changes. The storerooms had been properly shelved and partitioned out and Bridie knew exactly what was in them.

Then to the nursery where Mike had made no changes except for the bathroom and electricity, leaving everything else until he could consult with me. I prayed that he had not seen the almost invisible signature on the mural, and vowed to paint it out before Francis saw it and began to ask questions which I did not wish to answer.

Neither had I told my mother that her errant husband was alive and thriving in America with the wealthy wife, who was not legally his wife. His betrayal had been too terrible for her, and the memories of those dark days did not need reviving.

The family bedrooms were all completed and the bathrooms working. I was just so delighted with my own rooms. The sad stained wallpaper had been replaced by Chinese silk featuring beautiful birds perched on twigs or flitting between sprays of flowers. Pale celadon curtains and bedcover together with a cream carpet enhanced the room's elegance. The lovely room was reflected in the shining mirrors.

We agreed that the guest bedrooms on the opposite side must be left until later. Here was a man with the sense and experience to timetable the work realistically.

Downstairs we inspected each room in daylight, and made notes of anything that still needed attention or that I felt needed to be changed. Thankfully the making good of the plasterwork following the installation of the electricity cables had been skillfully done. The decorators had met with my mother, and matched the colours to those that she remembered.

The great hall was all splendour, and the floor tiles undamaged. We paused for coffee in my sitting room. The time had flown by, as our inspection and note taking had taken longer than expected.

Mike refused to be drawn on the closed library, saying that it awaited the arrival of Francis just prior to our wedding. Agreeing to resume the next morning we shook hands with mutual respect. He certainly looked surprised when I asked him if the roofs, chimneys and guttering had been inspected.

It was in the kitchen that the biggest changes had occurred. When I thanked the staff for their terrific efforts yesterday I had fallen back in amazement. The long table stood in its accustomed central place. Now it was surrounded by comfortable wooden chairs, not the long forms. The old range stood burnished, with copper kettles shining on its top. There were two quite large electric cookers, which I had only seen in magazines. There was a deep butler's sink and draining boards to save constant trips to the scullery. The walls, cupboards and dresser were all painted cream, so that the crockery looked fresher too. The large refrigerator was cook's pride and joy, and I am sure that she opened it for the sheer pleasure of doing so.

Bridie always provided small vases of flowers along the length of the table, so the whole effect was pleasing and homely, but efficient. I was amazed at the change in cook too. She had arrived as a temporary part-time morning help for Bridie, yet somehow had become a permanent full-time cook. Her apron and cap were spotless, and her delight in the new clean cookers, which she had soon adapted to was evident. Without the need for all the stoking of the old range with its dirt and soot she had more time to concentrate on the cooking and to improve her skills.

Promising to look in tomorrow to admire the still room, scullery, pantry and all the auxillary rooms, I took a cup of tea, water and a small sandwich to the small sitting room where it was time for my singing exercises. Like an athlete, a singer must train every day to keep their voice in top form. Having done so all my professional life I did not intend to stop now.

Every day was full of excitement and new discoveries. When I walked in the rose garden the perfume was intoxicating as the earlier blooms were in full glory. I had not seen it looking so well since I was a young housemaid.

I tried to peer through the curtains into the library for what woman is not curious, but they were tightly closed. I would just have to wait for Francis. I was growing impatient for our wedding day to arrive and to welcome him back to Courtneys.

After completing my inspection with Mike Roberts, which was to start much earlier, I was to meet with the staff to speed on with the wedding preparations. Bridie assured me that they were all well in hand.

The little pavilion in the rose garden from where Francis had first painted me had itself been painted. Now pale blue and white it looked like a little iced cake. I sat there quietly wondering why such a wealthy young man had come to England as a tutor. When I asked him he always said – 'to widen my horizons and to find you my darling'. Since the conversation always ended in a kiss or several that was the end of any further questions.

But now I had a mystery to solve.

When I took Miss Arabella's tea in I could tell that she had a searching question for me. I saw how important it was to her, so I listened carefully and kept my wits about me.

'Bridie when I inspected Sir Edward's old bedroom I was drawn to a small painting in the dressing room, which I had not seen before. I found it particularly beautiful and touching. I had recognised it at once as a John Hoppner, signed and dated. It featured two particularly charming children. One was a boy of about 6 years playing with a small black and white dog. His sister sat with flowers in her lap making daisy chains. One of these chains was around her neck, and the other crowning her fair hair. The boy was as dark as she was fair. His hair was in curls while hers fell straight to her shoulders. She was looking at both him and the dog with great devotion. The impact of the scene was at once beguiling, while the artist's skill in capturing the sunlight falling on the woodland glade was masterful.."

Arabella had found it entrancing, and searching for a wedding gift for Francis knew immediately that she had found it. But where had it come from?

I remembered the day well. While Evelyn sat on the bed describing the decoration and when the curtains had been installed.   I remembered that I had not cleared out the drawers at the bottom of the gentleman's wardrobe.   I would need to return and clear the clothing there.   Much of it would be too good to throw away and could go the Irish brothers of to the village. At the very back of the very last drawer, I had found a parcel wrapped in brown paper, tied with string and bearing a sealing wax impression of Sir Edward's seal. Opening it carefully in front of Evelyn, we discovered this little gem of a painting Evelyn had never seen it before either.

Could it be that when he was still able to holiday abroad he had bought it? Did he do so because it reminded him of his Grandchildren? Had he seen it in a London gallery and smuggled it back to Courtneys in his luggage? We would never know.

Miss Arabella's first thought was that it might be part of Richard's inheritance, and that she must return it to him. I reminded her that she had bought Courtneys 'Lock, Stock and Barrel'. The locks all needed oiling, the stock had been ravaged, and the barrel along with the wine cellar was empty!

Thus re-assured Miss Arabella relaxed.

Arabella wished Bridie to take, Edie, Millie and Maire to London in two days time with the shopping list, which they would compile tomorrow. They were not to return until they had each chosen an outfit for her wedding. Maire was to draw out cook at supper, and buy her something lovely, for had she not kept them all going with splendid food and drink during the months since Christmas?

Bella knew that Finch would wear the dress suit, which he had used at Christmas. Bella had one final surprise. The dresses, which Bridie and Maire were to select, were to be bridesmaids' dresses. Her former dresser could not contain her pride and happiness.

So it was that they needed to inspect the wedding dress hung up behind cotton covers in Arabella's wardrobe. At first she thought it too sophisticated, but its splendid lines were perfection, rather like Courtneys itself. Bridie and Maire were to aim for two dresses in pale green moire, which would highlight their titian hair, but if they found a dress which caught their hearts then it was to be their choice. A shopping list for Fortnum and Mason's was to go with Bridie; with the strictest instructions that she was to pay a hefty deposit and for the wedding cake in full. She was to obtain the assurance that the wedding cake was to arrive 5 days before the wedding and the more perishable items 2 days before. Thanks to Mrs Preston's famous new refrigerator they could be safely stored.

With this all agreed, Arabella walked down to the village to check that all was well with her Mother and Alice. Evelyn seemed a

little stronger and so happy that her dear daughter was to marry a
man of standing whom she really liked. He was honorable,
devoted to Arabella and his generosity was boundless.

Alice, who was 10 years younger than Evelyn, had travelled to
Cheltenham with their sister Celia to choose their wedding outfits.
Evelyn had asked them to bring for
her a lilac dress and hat to reflect her daughter's deep violet eyes.
Bella stayed for supper, and they spent a happy evening
discussing the wedding, for what else would they do? Bella
basked in the warmth of their loving approval. Is this how her
mother had felt before she married the feckless Sean? She had
asked them to spend the night before her marriage at Courtneys
so as to watch her getting dressed. Alice was to fix her veil and
headdress and act as her dresser for the last time.

Her staff had left for London breathless with excitement. They
returned laden down with parcels and breathless with exhaustion.
Cook had left cold meats, cheeses, pickles and bread and butter
for supper. So fortified with that and cups of tea they retired to
bed. They would tell of their adventures in the morning.

Cook and Miss Arabella could barely believe their ears. The shops
had been visited, the prices exclaimed at, the dresses and hats
tried on a quick lunch eaten so as not to waste time.

Then it all happened at once. Bridie and Maire were in the thick
of it, while the more cautious Edie and Millie hung well back. It
happened like this. As the four girls walked along the busy
Haymarket, the traffic was brought to a halt by a great phalanx of
marching women. They carried placards, which demanded

VOTES FOR WOMEN. Wearing mainly green, purple and white they marched determindly ignoring the catcalls of the nasty men.

Several police officers provided an escort, but when a man threw a missile, the woman it hit cried out in shock. Her fellow suffragettes turned on the culprit and Bridie, her Irish temper aflame shouted at him – 'You should be ashamed of yourself!'

In a flash police whistles blew and Bridie was seized but not the man who had caused the trouble. This enraged Bridie even more, and it was only when Maire insisted that Bridie apologised that she was released with a warning. Sobered by this turn of events the girls took a cab to the station, and set off for the safety of Courtneys. But the damage had been done. From here on Bridie who normally bowed to no man was to become an ardent and effective suffragette.

Fortified by many cups of tea, they put aside their London adventure. Each was given a list by Bridie of the work that needed to be done. They went down their lists asking for clarification if they saw a problem.

Beds were to be changed, final dusting polishing and primping to be done. The Irish lads brought in the tables to range along the sides of the hall. The glasses were polished and covered with clean cloths. A miscellany of pretty cups and saucers appeared together with the table for the wedding cake.

Everything that could be done early was completed. The drawing room, dining room and library windows were to be thrown open so that the guests could walk through into the garden. Here

Finch and his helpers would set up small tables and chairs, and everywhere there would be flowers. Just as Arabella was about to engage florists she saw a display, which Maggie Jones had done. No florist could have bettered it. It was agreed that Maggie would take charge of all the flowers, leaving Bridie free to supervise everything, before changing roles to become chief bridesmaid. Two extra maids had been engaged and an assistant cook and kitchen maids. 'Keep it simple, simple but best quality' Evelyn had advised.

The guest list had expanded despite her and Francis's wish for a small wedding. Aunt Celia and Uncle Jack had four children, some grown up and married, so that was eight guests from just one family. The villagers, tenants and staff would have a special celebration nearer to Christmas, when the happy couple returned from America. It would be a traditional ox roast with barrels of beer and all the
usual roistering to celebrate a wedding from the big house. Many understood that Miss Arabella wished to enjoy her wedding and depart for her honeymoon without a great deal of fuss.

There was disappointment that none of Francis's family were to be present. Everyone had hoped to see the mega-rich Americans with all their wealth and jewels on display. A huge reception at his American estate was not quite the same.

At least it saved her father having to make some inventive excuse. But only Arabella knew that.

Arabella had asked her mentor, Hugh Davenport, to give her away. He was travelling from London with Francis, her agent

Alfred Millard and Fitz, who had all done so much to establish and advance her career.

They were to stay the night before the wedding with the Richards, and Christopher was to act as Francis's Best Man. The two men had become friends; often riding together with Christopher supplying a mount for Francis. Bella thought this was noble of him as she suspected that he still had feelings for her, and to witness her marrying another man must sadden him.

With 5 days to go the cake arrived safely and was stored in the cool pantry ready to be set up the night before the wedding. The lists of work to be completed were diminishing rapidly. Flowers were ordered from Covent Garden so as not to denude Finch's borders, and more would be delivered at the Church for the flower arrangers there. 'The Order of Service' sheets were ready, the hymns chosen and organist and choir well rehearsed. They were rather nervous at the prospect of singing before Arabella and her guests, but when she dropped in at choir practice to thank them in advance she reminded them that she had first sung solo aged 10 in this very church with some of the self-same choristers. Her affability and evident excitement were cheering. The gift of luxury chocolates which would arrive the following week would be equally so.

Her mother and aunt now insisted that she leave the rest of the preparations in the capable hands of Bridie and the staff. It would not do for the bride to appear before her groom and the congregation tired out.

Her wedding eve saw Arabella as excited as any bride should be contented that all the preparations were complete.   The number of guests was indeed small for the marriage of a couple of such wealth and status, but just what the couple wanted.

Following a little time in the dusk shrouded rose garden Arabella went to bed early and slept softly and soundly.

My life has not quite turned out as I intended. I have spent long hours thinking over when it all changed – that is when I became capable of cohesive thought. I don't believe that I am bad, but I have certainly behaved with the most utter stupidity and made a hash of everything.

It all began with such promise I must have been a little over 4 when Nanny explained that Caro and I would have a new friend. Well we had all been waiting for a baby brother for ages, so perhaps he had arrived at last. It was a great surprise when Mrs Seymour of all people brought in a girl! She was called Arabella but since Caro couldn't say it we all called her Bella. I found out later that this was Italian for beautiful, and I suppose that she was. She had clouds of soft fair hair, and big eyes. I thought that she looked like one of the cherubs in our story books. She could already walk and toddled about annoyingly, tagging after Caro and me. I suppose we just got used to it really and I tried not to think of her as a pet dog. She could speak early too and then it was better. Bella soon stopped calling 'wait for me' because she was strong while Caro was often unwell with one childhood illness after another and in the end it was she who tagged behind.

I was indulged by Nanny and the nursery maids, because I was a boy and the heir to Courtneys.

When Caro and I were dressed up to go down to the drawing room to see Mama and Papa I always stood up very straight. They asked questions and I answered clearly. Mama was so lovely and gentle. She came up to the nursery before dinner to read us a story, embrace us and leave us with a kiss and a lingering smell of her perfume. Papa was kind in a manly sort of way. He smelt of tobacco for he smoked though Mama disapproved, and he never smoked in her presence. He would often take me on his knee and called me 'old chap', which I realised was a term of endearment.

The nursery was warm and cosy, and Nanny Bates was always there, keeping an eye on us, and ensuring that we minded our manners. I remember lots of warm or cool drinks, warm or cool clothing, and remembering to say 'thank you' to Ivy and Clara the nursery maids.

The three of us had lessons in the mornings from an early age because Papa was a strong believer in education. Mama also insisted that the management of a large house required girls to be equally well educated and not just decorative. Because I was older, I was at a different level, until once again Bella showed real promise and could read and write long before she left us to attend the village school and to live at her mother's cottage with her aunt. After our lunch rest Caro and I often used to collect her from the kitchen or housekeeper's room where she had been with her mother. Cook always managed to slip me a biscuit with a wink, and Ivy would laugh and look the other way.

We would run around in the gardens and when we found the clearing in the woods that we were sure was the one painted on the nursery wall we went there every day. We would chase butterflies and catch tadpoles or minnows in the little pool. Bella and I longed to climb trees but this was strictly forbidden in case we fell and injured ourselves. As we grew more adventurous the nursery maids were kept busy keeping an eye on us to ensure out safety.

For my eighth birthday Papa bought me my first pony. He was a sturdy little chestnut, who I was allowed to name. I was put up, and a groom led me round. I felt at once comfortable in the saddle and rode every day. Most children would have ridden from the age of five, but my father was mindful of our family history where James Courtney had established the famous stud, and Hugo had lost it with bad decisions and wild bets, did not wish me to become too attached to horses.

If only he had succeeded in that aim!

We only kept two carriage horses, two hacks, a pony for the trap, and now my Pebbles. Father was known in the County not to be a horseman, so never to ride to hounds or to even attend a steeplechase or point-to-point.

Those guests who saw the many paintings of the famous horses bred at Courtneys were surprised.

Grandfather, whom I seldom saw, would sometimes invite the three of us into the library. When the maid brought his tea and our drinks we would sit on the rug in front of the fire while he talked to us about the estate. Caro and I listened politely but it was Bella who gazed at him transfixed, by his aura of authority, for hadn't her mother always spoken of Sir Edward with the greatest respect?

When we got up to leave Bella walked around the bookshelves. Never had she dreamed that so many books could exist. However would anyone have time to read even a quarter of them? She marveled at the fine bindings on the spines, for she found out later that was how they were described. There were dark green, burgundy, light brown and deep chestnut brown. Some were almost black with age. Bella longed to run her fingers along them, but dare not touch. When she came to a tall wooden stand and saw the great book above her she turned to my Grandfather and said 'Please Sir Edward, what is that?' To our astonishment Grandfather opened the great folio and turned the pages until he found what he was looking for. Then he lifted Bella up to look at it. She cried out in wonderment and delight, and told us afterwards what she had seen. Thus was her first sight of the Audubon 'Book of American Birds' that great work which would bedevil my life in the future.

Grandfather set her down, led us to the door and returned us to Clara who was waiting in the hall to take us back to the nursery. I had hoped to slip away and see cook – but no luck.

Soon I was off to prep school, Bella to attend the village school and Caro to stay in the nursery and spend more time with Mama.

I did the least amount of work possible to make sure that I did not fluff my entry exams to Eton. Since Papa had gone there I was sure that I would get in.

Eton was a whole new experience. We younger boys fagged for the older boys whom we regarded as demi-gods. I loved any sport, and because I was tall and well made for my age did well at most of them. I loved rowing, cricket and athletics best of all. I was in all those teams when we beat Harrow easily. Although drunkenness was frowned on a blind eye was turned on these occasions for Harrow were the 'old enemy'.

Oxford was great fun. There were the rowing, cricket, rugby and athletic clubs. These were cliques reserved for the wealthy and the cricketing gods, and of course carousing and the wenching.

When I was down for the holidays at Courtneys, I noticed the new housemaid at once. Bella was at once beautiful and respectful. Like her mother she was efficient, but in no way servile. 'Good Morning Master Richard' greeted me at breakfast and I wished her 'Good Day'.

My 21st birthday had been the usual party for the great and the good. The tenants gathering, which followed it was a far more lively. affair. We had an ox-roast, all the farmers' wives brought mountains of food as well. Pa had been unstinting with the barrels of ale, for countrymen have a powerful thirst.

The fiddlers got going, and a country dance is much more fun than a formal one. I fetched up opposite Bella and swung her round with great energy. She was laughing and her hair was flying.

The heat and sparks from the ox-roast, the bonfire and the flaming torches seemed to inflame me. Never had I felt such desire. She must have been 17, and as I drew her close she looked at me with surprised eyes – those great eyes of hers – for my desire was quite obvious. For a moment I imagined a response, but then she was swept away in the dance. I never saw her again that night, and I slaked my desires with Farmer Watkins' buxom and willing daughter.

Pa had taken me to the stables. There awaited me the most wonderful horse I had ever seen. He was so black and shining with health and vigour. His conformation was staggering and at nearly seventeen hands he looked as if he could jump over the moon! We looked at each other with mutual inquisitiveness. Pa passed me an apple and as he lifted it from my hand and I stroked him, we formed a bond, which could never be broken.

I had the strongest feeling that I had seen his like before. Then it came to me for it was in one of the paintings of the Courtney stud horses. Its title was COURTNEY CAVALIER RAVENSWING. I preferred to call him just RAVEN.

I had been born in suspicious circumstances for my dam had not been covered. It was only when her owner noticed that the girth would not easily fasten, that he realised that she was in foal.

But how and where had she been covered? If she knew she was certainly not telling, but he caught her looking rather longingly at the five bar gate which secured her field. Could it be that a stallion had leapt it in order to serve her?

He awaited the birth of her progeny with some impatience for my colouring might give him some clue as to my sire. My birth was so difficult that it nearly did for my mother, but when I was up and nuzzling her she began to recover. Arthur Fletcher knew that she would never deliver a live foal again.

Because of the mystery of my birth, I was carefully nurtured.   I was an unusually sturdy foal and grew quickly as a colt; having strong bones and muscles and a pleasing conformation. Whoever my sire had been he must have been extremely handsome. Since my dam was a bay he must have been black, as I was too.

I was raised on Mr. Fletcher's farm where he had a reputation for breeding fine horses for the hunting field but very few in number. I grew up with his children around me and learned to treat them gently with sometimes three of them on my back. I was broken to the saddle with care and kindness and my spirit and temperament were undamaged.

It was when Sir Charles Courtney was visiting the farm that he first saw me. He must have retained his ancestors' keen eye for a promising young horse and at once knew that he had found a worthy gift for his son Richard.

It took much persuading and many guineas before I was taken to Courtneys. It was as though somewhere in my being I knew that I had come home. Richard at once knew that we would always have a special bond. He ran his hand down my neck, stroked my muzzle and offered me the most wonderfully tasty apple.

Our bargain to care for each other was struck. Whenever I could escape I would invade the kitchen garden in Autumn and strip the espalier tree where grew those most delectable apples. Old Finch went mad and shouted 'That dang blasted hoss', and proper blasphemous words. I didn't intend to flatten his blackcurrant bushes but they were in my path. I should have had colic, but I never did.

When I was old enough, strong and well-schooled over wide hedges and strong fences my Master took me to the hunt. He was mad for hunting like his ancestor, Sir Hugo, before him. He was such an accomplished rider, and I had such speed of foot that the Hunt Master often chided us for running ahead of him. At the steeplechase no one could beat us. I ran like the wind and leapt like a stag with my master low on my neck encouraging me onwards. He and his friends made many wagers, winning them all. In the end the odds were so low that no one would wager at all.

All was excitement and glory until in 1901 they were talking about

the death of Queen Victoria.   Far worse for us was the death of
Sir Charles Courtney, for then my master went mad!

Arabella awoke to the sun shining in through her window. How light and lovely the great house looked as if glorying in its renovations and care after the dilapidations of Richard's days.

Maire arrived with her breakfast tray. Bella at once noticed the most perfect rose in a small vase. Inhaling its perfume she presumed that it had come from Francis.

'This arrived this morning Miss Arabella. A gentleman delivered it and asked that you have this letter too!'

Good manners and a sense of what was right had caused Arabella to write to Richard. She offered to return the John Hoppner painting, which Bridie had discovered. The reply was brief. 'Thank you, but perhaps you may consider it some small recompense for the Audubons. I wish you happiness in your marriage' Richard.

So her wedding day began on a good note. As she enjoyed her breakfast Arabella remembered last night with a feeling of disbelief.

The travellers from London had all called at Courtneys for drinks and Irish cake. Hugh Davenport wanted to check on the duties involved in giving her away and all wanted to greet her and congratulate her. They all remarked on the wonderful changes to Courtneys.

With manicured lawns and borders, sparkling rooms and banks of

flowers, it did indeed look splendid. Francis drove them over to
the Richards and then returned for supper with Bella.

Taking her by the hand he led her to the door of the library,
produced the key, and unlocked the door. He did not switch on
the electric lights for the lamps all glowed and reflected on shelf
after shelf of books. Arabella flung herself into his arms.
'Oh darling it is absolutely wonderful. How on earth did you
manage it?'

'I've had my agents looking out for sales of books and Jarvis
alerted me – as you had asked him – of any local sales where
Courtney items were offered'.

'It's beyond words how wonderfully kind you are to me. I can't
begin to thank you. I just don't deserve you darling'.

'Maybe, but you're sure stuck with me! I could have given you
jewelry, but I know how much the library and books mean to you,
so believed that this would be the better idea'.

Turning, Arabella saw in the shadows that the stand now bore the
complete Audubon Book of American Birds. She cried out in
surprise, as Francis turned on the lights and the Great Golden
Eagle seemed to rise off the page and soar into life!

Arabella wept she was so overcome. Many exclamations
followed as she turned the huge pages fortified by a glass of
champagne. Bella toasted her husband to be with a full heart.
Now they must say 'Goodnight' for tomorrow would see them
joined in the 'Sight of God and in the face of this congregation' by

Revd. Peters. With a 'until tomorrow my love' she saw Francis out.

Then she returned to the library and sat for some time just gazing around. She felt such profound gratitude to Francis, and raising her glass toasted Sir Edward, for her vow to him was now completed.

The time just flew by until Bridie came in to dress Arabella's hair, which appeared more golden and luxuriant than ever. Bella applied her own make up for surely she had enough experience over the years.

The girls had been in total agreement as they had chosen their dresses and proudly entered in all their finery to help Arabella to don her bridal gown. Patou was world famous for simplicity, style and perfect cutting. To offset the sophisticated sheer satin, Aunt Alice had advised the simplest of satin slippers and flowers.

It was a huge disappointment that her mother and Alice could not be with her, but Evelyn had felt that the many stairs at Courtneys, together with the emotions of this longed for day might prove too much. She, Alice and Celia would all enter St Bart's just before Lady Cynthia and Caroline, and then the bride on Hugh's arm.

Thus it was that Bridie and Maire pinned the circlet of white roses into her hair. Her veil flowed from the back of her head since she declined to have it obscure her face.

Her bridesmaids preceded her down the great staircase, at the top Bella paused to think of all the brides before her who had set out with hope and love in their hearts. Perhaps there were some who did so out of duty alone.

Dear Hugh awaited her and whispered 'Dear girl you never made a better entrance or looked more beautiful'.
She kissed him gratefully, glad of his reassurance. The three bouquets awaited them in the cool of the Great Hall

This of course is where Archibald Finch had been so important, for it was to him that the provision of his finest roses for her hair and bouquet, and for the bridesmaids, had been entrusted. Maggie Jones had helped him to cut them, and with nimble fingers had converted them into headdresses and bouquets, simple but perfect.

The Richards had lent Bella their open carriage after it had taken them and their guests to the St. Bart's earlier. A chauffeur driven car had transported Francis and Christopher there, far too early, but Francis had insisted.

Paddy preceded them to the carriage, and handed them up. The girls helped to settle her dress and sat opposite to her and Hugh. As she thought how smart Hugh looked in his morning suit she felt a twinge of sadness that her father could not give her away. Then she remembered that he had chosen to be an absent father, whereas Hugh had been her mentor, adviser and yes friend, always promoting her career, and ensuring that she had the money to obtain her heart's desire, to own Courtneys.

There it stood golden and glowing, its every aspect pleasing. Spontaneously she blew it a kiss and Paddy, cook and the remaining staff waved to her.

Arabella could not believe that so many people had troubled to line the route to the Church. They waved and called out good wishes as the carriage passed by. Bridie and Maire waved back and smiled their wide Irish smiles, Hugh looked proud, and Bella quietly composed and delightful.

It was there as the carriage slowed to take the bend, which led up to the Church, that he stood bare headed. He bowed to her in respect, yet with the old quizzical look, which she knew so well. Bella acknowledged him with a grave nod and an almost shy smile. Thus a truce had been made between her and Richard.

Those villagers and well wishers who overflowed the Church waited to see the famous woman who had grown up among them. 'Isn't she beautiful' 'Isn't her dress lovely', and all the usual murmurings which accompany a bride to her wedding were heard.

The Minister awaited her, and with her bridesmaids following dutifully behind her they proceeded at a stately pace down the aisle. The organ thundered out a triumphant 'Entrance of the Queen of Sheba' for who could better escort her than Handel? Level with her beloved Mother who had always believed so strongly in a golden future for her 'Golden Child', Bella paused to take her hand.   A look of such love passed between them that those who saw it remembered it always.

Then Hugh delivered Arabella to the side of her bridegroom and Francis was totally dazzled. At that moment the sun struck a section of the stained glass window and seemed to cast a halo around her head. Thus it was that they 'plighted their troth' with the words of the great marriage ceremony with its holy vows. The choir sang melodiously and the congregation joined in the hymns enthusiastically. Then came the only anthem which Arabella and Francis could have chosen – 'I know that My Redeemer Liveth', for had Evelyn not brought up her daughter to believe that this was an unquestionable truth?

Bella and Francis exchanged their vows and were pronounced 'Man and Wife together'.

They left to the strains of Handel's 'Water Music' and 'Music for the Royal Fireworks' exploded as the congregation followed them out.

Of course there had to be some photographs and the press had got wind of the marriage but behaved quite politely. The bells rang out, and rose petals were cast as they entered their carriage, the happiest of couples for the drive back to

Courtneys. They waved and smiled and it was only the pressure of Francis's hand, which reassured Bella that it was not all some wonderful dream.

Bridie and Maire skipped in escorted by the Best Man. Hugh arrived with her Mother and Alice and the guests crowded in, though a special space was made for Lady Cynthia and Caroline as they entered their old home.

Seats of honour were provided for them and for the three sisters.

Champagne of the finest quality was served. Unusually the cake was cut, the speeches made and the toast drunk before the buffet was served.

Arabella and Francis had decided on this so that her mother should not become overtired. Paddy and Liam would take her and Alice home, and any other guests who needed to slip away with just a brief 'Thank you' could do so.

The toasts raised were short but no less affecting because of that. Tradition demanded that Hugh spoke 'In parentis', then Christopher rather nervously toasted 'The lovely bridesmaids' with his eyes firmly fixed on Bridie. Francis recalled his first visit to Courtneys so many years ago, and thanked everyone for making him so welcome on his return to claim his beautiful bride.

Then Arabella now divested of her veil rose. 'It may not be usual for the bride to speak at her own wedding, but I cannot let this wonderful day pass without thanking all of you who have made it possible. To Hugh, Alfred and Fitz who have steered my career. To Lady Cynthia who let me work and here and first allowed me to sing. To Caro, who has been my friend since childhood. To Edie, Millie, cook, Bridie and Maire and the brothers Noonan, who never seem to stop working. To John and Mike who have stopped me from making even more mistakes. To Mr Finch and Maggie who are such garden specialists – especially with roses. To my Aunts Celia and Alice and to the lady to whom I owe so much,
my Mother. Finally to the greatest piece of luck any woman can have, to my dearest husband Francis. To you all, and to a future to match its past for it has left its mark on all of us – to

COURTNEYS.'

Toasts were drunk, tears were shed, then the buffet was admired and attacked with vigour. It spread out into the garden where Finch was in his element showing the guests around, and dazzling them with the botanical names of all his plants.

There the strawberries and cream, trifles, elegant gateaux and tea were served. Cook and her helpers and Bridie wondered how so few people could eat so much, but felt that it reflected the excellence of the food they had provided.
It had been quite a day!

I had become very aware that Christopher Richards had become 'taken' by me. He drove over to Courtneys regularly always with a ready excuse each time to see me. While flattered, I realised that there could be no future for us, for his family would never consent to him marrying a Catholic girl however much it needed a transfusion of new and vigorous blood.

I was greatly amused to notice Christopher bringing a dish of strawberries to Caroline Courtney, who was now 30 and although beautifully dressed was pale and droopy. Now she appeared a little flushed and animated and at least she is acceptable to his family.

I have my eyes – my twinkling Irish eyes – on a very intriguing man.

Because of my position at Courtneys, when Mike Roberts arrived from America to take charge of the builders, it was necessary for us to consult on many occasions. I liked his practical approach and asked him many questions. These he answered with clarity and patience, so that I fully understood the provision of effective water supplies, water closets and central heating pipes. He had a firm understanding of the requirements of a large house, especially its domestic offices. Cook positively beamed as they discussed the merits of electric cookers and refrigerators.

The laundry maids, who came in for 2 days each week and had the hardest job of all, were excited beyond measure to hear of the new electric washing machine which was already sweeping

America and Mike would ensure reached Courtneys as soon as possible. Mike brought news of the New World with so many wonderful modern inventions.

I made very sure that Mike saw me in all my finery, for Maire and I made a pretty pair. While I needed to keep an eye on events, we had hired in plenty of extra staff to help.

It was a great day altogether, as there is much kissing and well-wishing at a wedding, I managed to plant a kiss full on his lips which shook him up a bit I could tell.

Maire had packed Miss Arabella's trunks. There were the ones for her honeymoon in Switzerland, then there were the ones to be loaded at Cherbourg, for the honeymoon couple were to sail straight on to New York. After that they would travel to Mr. Francis's family estate to meet all his family. They were to hold a great reception to celebrate the marriage of the heir to the Grantley fortune. He had taken his time choosing a wife, but as she was world famous, it was judged to be a splendid match.

I did feel a little envious of Maire, but I was needed at Courtneys and I had warned my sister that she was to miss nothing, remember everything and share it all with me when they returned.

Sadly this was to be much sooner than any of us expected!

What a grand weddin' it were!

There we were all dressed up in us best to see that grand lass wed. When Miss Arabella cum into old St Bart's wi' old Sid on the organ thunderin' away, an us all cranin' to see the bride it were great. The sun gave her a sort o' golden glow like one o' me best roses.

Talkin' o' roses that were when I got to be important. I were up at dawn to cut 'em while the dew were still fresh on the petals. Maggie wanted white for Miss Arabella, an' carmine for Bridie and Maire. Then she sat in the cool workin' away an' not speakin'. Ah took 'er a cup o' tea to keep er goin.

When ah saw them bouquets an' garlands ah were proud enough to bust. Better than any o' them posh London flowers, an' all the better for bein' Courtney roses for a Courtney bride an' when Miss Arabella mentioned us in 'er speech well weren' that summat?

O' course them toffs walked round me gardens wi' their glasses o' champagne. I ad' one an' all to show that ah'd bin' invited. They were well impresses that Maggie an' me knows all the botanical names. Talk about blindin' 'em wi' science. That showed 'em!

I'd got my eye on Mike Roberts. I fancied him and I fancied moving to America with him. When Miss Arabella toured there I always explored the cities we visited when she was busy. I'm a lively Irish lass always up for a bit of fun and a laugh. The bustle and their accents and the out and out energy of the folk suited me. I'd hoped to impress him at the wedding. Mike had never seen me looking pretty and pert with my lovely sea-green dress and flowers in my hair. It might have been different if they'd had dancing and I could have got close to him. Naturally Bridie got to him first and I saw the way he looked at her.
So that's that!

We'll be back in America soon for Miss Arabella and Mr Francis's big family reception there. Wait till they see her in all her finery. All her trunks are packed which kept me busy for she's a wealthy lady and must always look perfect. Then we've got to finish her tour before Christmas too. Give Mr Francis his due for he's never tried to stop her singing, though he'll get some funny looks from some folk.

We are off tomorrow to take the boat train to France then on to Switzerland. They'll want to be together every minute, so Frank Lewis who's Mr Francis's valet and me will travel together. He's not a very interesting chap but we'll rub along.
I've got a secret assignation!

The guests will all have left by 6 o'clock. Miss Arabella – no it's Mrs Francis now – has ordered a light supper in the library cos they were too excited to eat at their wedding feast. Then all the staff are going to sneak into the vegetable garden with Maggie and Finch and we'll finish off the food and drink.

The Irish lads and the older chaps will bring beer and Guiness for them.   We girls will polish off the wine.   We're meant to be quiet about it.   Some hopes with Paddy, Liam, Micky and old Finch when they get singing!   Millie will stay behind to answer the bell and serve supper.   She's Methodist and teetotal.

Then we'll creep up to bed so that the new Mr and Mrs Grantley can have Courtneys to themselves.

It's been a smashing day.

How do you describe the perfect day except to say that it was perfect?

Happiness is supposed to be catching and for Francis and me there seemed to be an epidemic. We shall both remember it until our last day on earth.   So simple, so relatively small in number, but swelled by the villagers and tenants.

Wonderful friends, wonderful service, wonderful flowers, wonderful food and sunshine everywhere glinting from my ever wonderful Courtneys. Waves and smiles and music – just delicious.

It was the greatest surprise to see Richard as I drove to church, but we acknowledged each other.   With the letter and the rose he had begun to redeem himself.

Amongst all the happiness two worrying events took place. My dear mother was in her place in church looking altogether charming in pale lilac, but also smaller, dwarfed by the pillars and majesty of St. Bart's.

Then during our reception Hugh managed to take me to one side. 'I know that you are worried about your mother Arabella and I have a suggestion to make. Suppose that after your visit to Francis's family instead of resuming your tour you return to England?
I have someone in mind to replace you. You could keep an eye on Evelyn and come to London regularly. I want you to rehearse

and then perform as CARMEN. It is a role you may not have considered, but I've been thinking it would be perfect for you now. It's passionate, provocative and sensuous and you'll carry it off splendidly. You'll have to take dance lessons as well, for that is central to the role. What do you say?'

The fact that Hugh recognised the change in Evelyn troubled Arabella. She kissed his cheek in gratitude for his consideration, accepting gratefully. Dear Hugh.

The guests left with the usual protracted goodbyes and good wishes. Alice and Evelyn had slipped away earlier, with looks of such love and happiness that Arabella's heart overflowed.

She and Francis changed into more casual clothes and took their tea into the 'iced cake' summerhouse. Gravely Francis handed her a letter. So many emotions! At first surprise, then disbelief, then an acceptance followed by the most radiant delight, for had not her new husband been the man to make Courtneys whole again?

The letter was from the Trustees informing her that an offer had been made for the Courtneys Estate in its entirety. This had been accepted, and it had been transferred to Arabella to mark her marriage to Francis. If she needed any reminder of his great wealth it lay in her hands. How could she ever show her gratitude for ensuring her heart's desire to heal and restore Courtneys?

In his turn Francis had as his wife the girl he had first known so long ago, but now his very beautiful wife. Would it be too fanciful to ask her to sing a lullaby for him this evening?

There remained one last item in the Trustees letter. It was their decision to hand the proceeds of the sale to MR RICHARD COURTNEY immediately, and so discharge their duties.

Later, as they ate supper and talked of the day's events their anticipation and desire for each other mounted. Their previous intimacies, delightful though they had proved to be, were now to be sublimated into the different coupling as man and wife.

At length after a final brief stroll in the rose garden they ascended the great staircase, and thence savoured their delight and passion as —

MR AND MRS FRANCIS GRANTLEY
Whether a lullaby was sung is doubtful!

'Oh me feet are fair killing me. Ah they're really sore but it were worth it.' Ethel Preston counted her blessings every day. She had started work at Courtneys as a part-time cook to help Bridie as she and the two maids tried to put things to rights after Master Richard's neglect.

The two slovenly maids had slung their hooks when Miss Arabella had bought the house. It was the talk of the whole village especially as she was so famous now and Evelyn Seymour so respected.

Anyhow I'd do the breakfasts, get a lunch that they could eat quickly, and leave the dinner prepared. By then they were so hungry that my good plain food was just what was wanted.

Before long Miss Arabella asked me to work full time, paid me on the dot, and it were better than stopping at home all day.

That old nuisance Archie Finch was everlastingly in after tea and biscuits. He calmed down when Maggie Jones started, and she fetched the tea herself. The builders had to fend for themselves in the stable block.

The girls were ever so hard working, and Bridie helped me with some recipes when I got stuck.

It got even better when Mr. Roberts came over from America, and them builders soon knew who was boss. He might have some funny ideas but they all make life easier.

First I had to have a new fangled refrigerator so the meat and fish and my fruit jellies all kept a treat. Every time I open my fridge I'm happy. I'd read all about

them electric cookers as well 'cos neither Lady Cynthia nor Miss Arabella would employ anyone who couldn't read or write and now I've got two to work with. The cookers all looked right smart, and to think no lighting 'em or stoking 'em, and no soot either.

Mr. Roberts wouldn't let them take the old range out. Black leaded and shone up with the copper kettles sitting on top it does look a treat. I've got proper running water and a good deep sink and two cookers for when we want to entertain.

Mike believed in being prepared, and when he came into supper the girls all perked up – and my cooking improved no end.

There was a bit of an upheaval with the scullery being done out and the stillroom as well as the pantries and the storerooms. Best of all he wouldn't allow any coal or coke stores to open into the scullery now that we don't need coal or coke for the range.

So that's how I came to be cooking in me smart cream kitchen with an assistant cook and extra maids to help for the wedding. Bridie and Maire were bridesmaids, and Edie and Millie invited guests. I couldn't even go to the church as I was so busy but I didn't mind.

They all came down for me to get a close look at their outfits – splendid it was and I knew those titian haired Irish lasses would choose sea green.

The rest of us all went up into the hall to see Miss Arabella leave with Mr. Hugh.   She fair took your breath away she's that beautiful.   Never a fairer bride left Courtneys in 200 years.   Mr. Francis is a lucky man.

It turned out to be a beautiful sunny day and warm too, but that's where my refrigerator comes in.   The hampers had arrived from Fortnum and Mason with every luxury food known to man – or woman.

Bridie and Jean, the new maid, worked out where everything must go, and Maire placed all the dishes and stands ready. They're right handy those girls and because they're used to making ladies look smart and pretty, they can do the same with food and flowers.

I was all set in my new uniform, which was a gift from Miss Arabella, and away we went.   There might have been only 60 guests but they ate and drank for England.   Then they took in the dining room and drawing room on their way through to the gardens for the desserts.   I felt right proud for I'd come a long way from being a 'jobbing cook' and was well satisfied with my efforts.

I'll bet it won't be anymore special at that big posh do for hundreds in America.

My wedding night was all that I had hoped and desired. My silk nightdress was just clingy enough, my hair loose and carefree, and the lamplight flattering for perhaps at 28 and 38 Francis and I were a little older than many couples. What passes between husband and wife should remain discreetly hidden. Shall I just say that after a surprising initial shyness we slipped back into the previous intimate understanding of each other's needs quite easily and delightfully.

Entirely content we took breakfast together. Francis had a last meeting with Mike Roberts to confirm the work to be done during the months that we were to be away. John Jarvis was to remain as Estate Manager. Following Sir Charles's death he had struggled on with no support from Richard. He managed to keep the estate going through the agricultural down turn until it was due to be transferred from the Trustees back to Richard.

Now with a new owner and with both Francis and I showing a keen interest and capital to invest, all augured well for the future. He did not intend to advise extravagance, but new investment was sorely needed.

We said goodbye to our staff to leave for the station with Maire and Frank Lewis following behind with our luggage. We had left time to call at the cottage to bid farewell to Evelyn and Alice.

Mother and daughter were left alone as Alice walked Francis to the gate, confiding her fears to him. Bella embraced her mother with a kind of fierce tenderness.

' I can't thank you enough for your wonderful care – you have been the truest mother anyone could imagine.'

'Darling girl I knew on the day of your birth that you were exceptional, and it is so. Be happy my dear.'

Those were the last words that her mother would ever speak to her. Thankfully Arabella was unaware of that.

The journey to Switzerland was uneventful and extremely luxurious, with any likely problems smoothed away.   They arrived in Geneva ready to enjoy that delightful city. Arabella had stayed there on one of her concert tours. She had loved the lake with its pretty steamers, and the snow-capped mountains. It really did look like a tourist brochure and was a mecca for walkers, climbers, naturalists and yes, for honeymooners.

Their suite overlooked the lake and they preferred to breakfast on the balcony before setting off on the day's exploration. Two weeks of mutual interest and happiness flew by. It was midway through their third week that the telegram arrived from Mike Roberts.

Francis was prepared, but not Arabella. The news of her mother's death was shattering, yet she knew that she had felt fearful for many months. Evelyn would have told her to 'Bear up, keep busy' for they were both practical women.

Bella asked Francis to walk with her through to the city's Cathedral where he left her.

Arabella knew what she must do. Making herself known, she asked that an organist be found for her. Thus she sang to a virtually empty Cathedral the great words of 'Ave Maria' with that rich full voice which her mother had fought so hard for her to develop. Her God-given talent transfixed all those who heard her. Francis, now seated at the back heard every word and thought his heart would break for her.

He realised how lucky he was to be married to Arabella with her high courage and determination. Who else could possibly have conceived the idea of saving Courtneys? Yet here she was singing with such tenderness and sadness for the woman she honoured. Their bond had been unbreakable, even with Evelyn dead there was the knowledge that somehow her presence and comfort would be there.

Together they returned to the hotel to prepare for their early morning departure for England.

Francis's family who were eagerly awaiting their arrival would have to wait again.

So it was that Evelyn's death happened when she was so contented.   She and I had lived together in sisterly accord since both of us had retired.

I had relinquished touring with Arabella with some relief when she was established and needed my advice less.   Bridie was a forthright and capable Irish lass and far quicker than me at costume changes and sewing.   Not better, just quicker.

Once Evelyn had seen Lady Cynthia and Miss Caroline settled in the Dower House she retired as well.   We led a quiet enough life, though I was busy teaching sewing in the school, and we both were active in the Church.

We always waited for Arabella to return from her travels with keen interest.   She seemed so driven once her legacy from Sir Edward had been destroyed by Richard.

Evelyn was quietly delighted when her daughter became mistress of Courtneys where she herself had spent the majority of her own working life.

At the same time we both realised what a huge task Bella had set herself working for four years flat out to buy it, and now funding the renovations.

All of us were immensely relieved when she became engaged to Francis who Evelyn remembered from his days as the young tutor at Courtneys.   The size and brilliance of Bella's engagement ring caused us believe that he was hugely wealthy.

When Francis sent Mike Roberts to take control of the work at Courtneys it was the greatest relief. Now our dear girl has married that splendid man. Following their wedding we spent a great deal of time remembering it fondly in the smallest detail. But Evelyn became tired so quickly, and when I went to wake her I realised that she had died in her sleep.

Now Arabella and Francis with Maire and Lewis were on their way back from Switzerland, with their honeymoon memorable for all the wrong reasons.

Bridie, Mike Roberts and I had started the funeral arrangements to make it easier for Bella. When they arrived back Arabella was pale but totally composed. She had gained this composure in Geneva Cathedral where her tears had been shed and her prayers for her mother said.

Bella wanted the funeral to take place as quickly as possible. This time, so shortly after her own glorious day, the skies were dark and overcast. The carriages were drawn by black horses.

We set off from Courtneys as it gave its faithful servant her final send off. The people who lined the route stood bare headed and bowed as the cortege passed by.

The resonant and time honoured words of the burial service proceeded. The Revd. Peter's tribute and address were brief but fitting. The choir and congregation sang the great hymns chosen by Arabella. No anthem was sung, just the TE DEUM, the choir formed a guard of honour for the coffin of its long serving member.

Evelyn's earthly remains were interred in the Church burial ground. A small wake was held in the church hall, for Bella could not bear to host everyone back at Courtneys so soon after her wedding reception.

When Arabella and Francis arrived back from the funeral, Bella went at once to bed. Bella confided later that Bridie had brought her those great comforters, hot tea and toast with a small tot of brandy. Curled up in her own bed she fell at once into an exhausted sleep. When she awoke it was to find a fire burning in the grate – for it was a cold evening – while the room was softly lit with lamps and candles.

Francis sat alongside the bed holding her hand, and gazing at her with such loving concern that she wept. Thus folded in her husband's arms and sheltered within the walls of Courtneys she was safe. Then she slept again, and when she awoke it was to a new bright day.

After the breakfast there was only one place that Francis and Bella wanted to visit. As they walked in the rose garden Finch appeared. Doffing his cap to her he made almost courtly bow and presented her with the most glorious golden rose of such intense form and perfume that Arabella gasped with pleasure.
'Oh Mr Finch it's divine.'
He drew himself up proudly and announced
'Ah've done it at last! It's taken me years, but ah've done it at last! It's to be named MISS ARABELLA'

Looking at him with tears of gratitude in her eyes she said
'My Dear Mr Finch could we perhaps name it
"Sweet Evelyn"?'

AND SO IT WAS

Chapter 46   Richard   1908

When I was called before the Trustees I knew that something was afoot. It had been seven very long years since I had inherited Courtneys. Then I wagered, drank, gambled and wenched away all the proceeds from the contents.

I was forced to sell to an anonymous buyer who turned out to be Arabella Seymour.

I now had 3 more years on a measly allowance before I could realize the whole estate. Give the Trustees and old Jarvis their due for they had kept it in good order, so that it would be worth quite a deal of money when I at last inherited.

Perhaps Pa and Grandfather had been right when they so curtailed me. I had hoped to be chosen to either run or row in the London 1908 Olympics. A bad fall while out hunting put a stop to those ambitions, so I was rather drowning my sorrows.

The Trustees had a proposal to put before me. They had received an offer on the estate, which was too good to refuse. Would I agree to allow them to accept it and to terminate their duties? Would I just! Looking serious I asked them for the value of said offer. When they told me I had the greatest difficult not to leap into the air in elation. Consent given and duly signed, they did have two suggestions for me. That I invested the money and lived on my hugely increased income, and that I set up a home of my own in a more modest but still gentlemanly way.

I told them that I would consider both suggestions very seriously indeed and discuss them with Mama. I did rather tend to drop in on her when I needed a bed, or a meal or money or all three.

I listened to her advice and bought a small manor house setting up an establishment with stables. With several grooms and an efficient indoor staff I began to settle down at last. I no longer raced Raven after his ruinous loss in the steeplechase where he had been beaten when I had exhausted him the previous day, and had other horses to hunt with. Because of my prowess on the hunting field there was talk of putting me up for Master. This, however, I gracefully declined.

It had been a precarious few years and I determined to do better, and to perhaps marry. I need to safeguard the Courtney line, for it was now clear that Caroline would never marry.

I was touched to receive Arabella's startling letter on the eve of her wedding, offering me Grandfather's Hoppner painting. My answer declining her offer was the Audubons were worth considerably more, together with the rose tribute was gentlemanly. I know that her new husband greatly exceeds her in wealth and standing in America, but even so he's a lucky dog. She really is quite spectacular.

I hear that Mrs. Seymour is dead and that Bella and her husband leave for America as soon as possible.

Meanwhile I shall ride daily – dear old Raven – and hunt and shoot in season. I shall walk Beaner and Bosun every evening and endeavour to stifle my constant desire for alcohol, which ruined me before and will do so again if I weaken.

146

I have cut off all my former drinking and gambling friends and manage to pour away the stirrup cups.   I seldom go out in company and this removes me from temptation.

I still have two great desires – for alcohol and for Arabella!

Chapter 47   Francis and Arabella   1908

Our voyage back to America was uneventful, with calm seas, blue skies and brisk breezes. I was aware of the mixture of sunshine and showers in Arabella. Actress that she was no-one among the passengers would have guessed of her inner turmoil.

We breakfasted in our suite, walked the decks holding hands, dined and danced as all newlyweds do. Her poise was undisturbed, her outfits, whether for deck or dining room, well chosen, and of the latest fashion as befits a star and trend-setter.

Each afternoon saw her engrossed in her voice exercises, which she took even more seriously now that Hugh Davenport had offered her Carmen. Only Maire and I saw the sadness in her eyes. Her mother had died aged 71, and Bella was unsure whether Sean, who had been the great love of her mother's life, had brought her joy or pain. Perhaps both in equal measure.

On the final evening Bella asked me to take her up on deck and to leave her there. Feeling anxious I stood in the shadows. To my astonishment she gazed out to sea and sang 'The Skye Boat Song'. At length she turned away, and as I moved towards her she came into my arms. I felt that all the tension had disappeared, almost as if she had waved goodbye at last to Evelyn.

When we docked the following day, all was hustle and bustle on the quay. A car took us to our hotel, while Maire and Lewis waited to supervise our luggage. We were only to stay one night in New York, as I was anxious to travel to FAIRHAVEN and my expectant family as soon as possible. Although they had met her on her famous Sunday visit, I longed to present Arabella as my wife and my love.

American trains are just great, and as all men become overgrown schoolboys around them, then great fun too. Once aboard and settled in our compartment we were free to watch the countryside speed by, visit the dining car or the observation car, and we did all three.

Our travelling bags were in a separate compartment so that Maire and Lewis could supply the appropriate outfits whenever needed. I strongly believe in comfortable travel to lessen the fatigue of it.

When we arrived at the station nearest to Fairhaven, we were met by two cars to transport us all and, at the house, by all the family. Amid merry chatter I proudly introduced Arabella to them as my wife!

It was such a wonderfully happy time for me and I was so proud of my beautiful girl. Nothing would satisfy Bella more than a walk with Ma in her famous garden. Gardens might be nearer the mark, as they were so extensive and varied. Many vistas and unusual plant varieties were admired. Whilst Arabella and my mother toured the gardens I sat in the shade and considered my good fortune to have such blessings bestowed on me – my background, my family, and Arabella until we were called into lunch, which was served with some ceremony and greatly enjoyed.

My family are an amiable and sometimes eccentric lot. At its head is my father, RANDOLPH. He is powerful both physically and in business. He believes in paying a good day's pay for a good day's work. Armed with this principle and mindful of the well being of his workers, he ensured that schooling, healthcare help for them and their families, along with good housing, was on offer. I suppose in that way he was a philanthropist like Cadbury and Fry in England.

No one ever took him for a pushover. He struck a mean bargain, but his word was his bond. He led a huge conglomerate of businesses and was totally
respected in the mining, engineering, steel work, manufacturing plants and factories which he ran so successfully.

Part of that success was due to his insistence that his managers got their hands dirty before they reached the boardroom. Fully on top of the business himself he required them to be able to answer his questions, and to present a case and stand up for the sections. If anyone within or outside his empire tried to 'Do him down' as he expressed it, and were not straight with him, he made it his business to see that they neither worked for him again, nor retained any sort of good character thereafter. I suppose that he was one the great 'Captains of Industry', who had driven America into such prominence in the world, and I was rightly proud of him.

Power is a powerful attraction and he might well have become Randy by name and randy by nature. I've been told that he was always surrounded by beautiful girls trying to catch a big fish, and a rosy future. However he was fortunate to meet a girl who was not beautiful – but merely pleasant looking. She was neatly but not extravagantly dressed, and made no effort to flirt or make

eyes at him. However she held one overriding attraction for him –
she was hugely intelligent. As he came to know her, and then to
court DOROTHEA MAYBELLE STANWELL, my father met a mind
equal to his own, though with different objectives. That lady
became my Mother. Her days were not spent with dressmakers
or milliners.   A day where she did not garden or paint or read or
attend a lecture or a library or art gallery was no day at all. She
felt herself to be the equal of any man, except in physical
strength, but wisely did not boast of this.

Once, over dinner, whilst reminiscing, my mother told us that
when my father proposed to her she had told him quite matter of
factly-
'I have come to love you and should be honoured to be your wife
– however – I must tell you there is a caveat.   Should you ever
betray me with another woman whatever the circumstances or
excuse, I shall immediately leave you, taking with me any children
we may have.   This you must accept and assure me of.'

My father laughed and then added that he knew a bargain when
he saw it and hastened to announce their engagement and
forthcoming marriage but that in his turn had a request for his
fiancée.
'I know how much you dislike big society events, but I will need
you to accompany me, especially as you are such a brilliant
conversationalist and people queue up to talk to you.   I really
detest the ballet and opera.   The theatre and an art exhibition are
tolerable, but please I beg you do not ask me to escort you to any
evenings of torture.'
We laughed and at this end agreed that these terms had been
honoured ever since.

Apparently a deal was struck with a handshake and a kiss. Their marriage was fruitful in every way. Mother did not try to reign in his ambitions, and Father gave his support to her love of portraiture, which rather like Topsy grew and grew. I knew she always showed him a portrait before purchasing it, and that he learned to keep quiet if he thought it moderate so that on occasion when he burst out 'Gosh, that really is horrible, surely you do not mean to buy something so dead ugly' wisely Mother did not do so!

It was imperative that the company had large offices in New York, which was for Randolph the centre of the universe, with branch offices near to his many businesses. Dorothea could not bear to live in a big city so they bought an estate in the countryside and stayed in hotels when Randolph needed to be away for too long. FAIRHAVEN has been our home ever since.

In due time they were blessed by three children. First was myself, Francis, followed by Annette and Phillipa. We all grew up healthy, well formed, well educated and well mannered. I think it is a truism that nothing works out quite as intended. I grew up to be somewhat intense, committed to my books, my

sketching and I was devoted to my parents. By the time I returned from England, after my stint as tutor to the children of an English knight , I was adjudged to have 'Got it out of his system' by my Father and to have 'Realised his ambitions' by my Mother, a very good outcome I believe.

As the company would need a family member at its head once my father retired, so Francis it had to be! Realising that acquiescence would be to my advantage, and anxious to help to protect the family businesses, I buckled down. I know I became valuable as the one who always had a clear overview of the situation.

It may have come as a surprise to Father when each of his daughters eschewed the usual pastimes of rich young women. Annette developed a fascination with aircraft. She learned the intricacies of a plane's engineering, and became a bold but safe flyer. CHECK, CHECK and CHECK again was her mantra before take-off, hence she always landed safely. My father often wondered how long it would be before she wanted to establish a Grantley Aero Division?

Phillipa became the family's motoring expert. Both sisters did tend to wear overalls, and with cap or helmet and goggles fooled many into thinking that they were chaps, which amused us hugely. The two men who were astute enough to penetrate their disguises became their husbands, and Luke and Simon joined the family.

I was roused from my reveries by the call to lunch, which no doubt would be served with some ceremony and to be greatly enjoyed. The final few members who had been introduced were my Aunt Hilary and her husband Steve, then Aunt Penelope and her husband Sean. Did I imagine a slight hesitation on Bella's part as Uncle Sean kissed her in greeting? Perhaps not!
We all separated after lunch for a rest. Tea was served on request and wherever in the house or grounds, in two's or four's, or any other number, before we all met again for dinner.

I had been given an extra week of honeymoon leave by the company, so as to show Bella the estate and the surrounding countryside. We took a picnic and I took the wheel. There was a very substantial estate to show her. In the early fall sunlight the land glowed.

Accustomed to the smaller vistas of the English countryside, Bella was overwhelmed by the huge space and expanse before her, and now understood how America was becoming so dominant in world agriculture. Our lead in automobile technology was reflected in farm machinery. With world wide demand for tractors and harvesters proving to be insatiable America was indeed great.

FAIRHAVEN itself was majestic. All white, with colonial pillars to mark its entrance and status. Its façade seemed to stretch forever and return wings provided spacious accommodation for family, guests and staff. It was run with almost military precision and efficiency, yet so unobtrusively that only the staff and Dorothea were aware of it. Her girls were far to busy with their aeroplanes and automobiles to show the slightest interest in the house. Phillipa, Penelope and Hilary were on so many charity committees that they were engrossed elsewhere. As long as their usual comforts were available everyone was content.

Arabella of course knew how much effort was required to keep such a large undertaking afloat. She used to love walking through the grand rooms admiring Dorothea's great good taste. So many American homes and hotels could be a little overblown, but at Fairhaven all was understated but of the highest quality. There were pieces of Chippendale and Adam, at whose cost Arabella trembled. There were magnificent carpets and curtains, wonderful paintings of course with Sevres porcelain and Paul de Lamerie and Paul Storr silver. Neither too much nor too flamboyant, I felt it spoke of great wealth, great comfort and great good taste.

The ballroom had been designed for grand entertaining. It had been newly decorated in palest blue with matching floor length curtains. There were long mirrors over pier tables to reflect the four huge chandeliers. It was all designed to add glitter and sparkle to the dancers as they dipped and swirled around the floor.

The orchestra, florists and caterers were all booked for the great reception which Ma and Pa were giving to celebrate our marriage.

All was in place and I surmised on the day many ladies spent much time with society hairdressers. Not Ma and Arabella of course. It was so easy for us men to don evening dress with good studs and cufflinks. The ladies would be expected to put on a show, which would reflect their status and that of their partners.

Ma had quietly asked Arabella if she might consider singing for everyone. Faced with so much care taken for our reception how could she refuse? An accompanist and the music, which she requested had appeared as if by magic two days before, so Bella felt well rehearsed and confident. She was experienced enough to know that the pianist from the orchestra was perhaps not equipped to play for a classical singer. Entries and tempo are all important. How she longed for 'Fitz' O'Brien. However she found Mr. Allard to her liking and vowed to use him for her engagements if 'Fitz' was unavailable.

At last all the vehicles of the suppliers had left. The house was ablaze with lights and the orchestra was tuning up, ready to play as the guest arrived.

I was just checking my bow tie when my wife entered. Arabella's eyes seemed to be more brilliant than ever and shone with excitement. She and Maire had decided that simplicity would outshine excess. She wore a Fortuny dress of the finest pleated golden silk, so that she appeared to float as she walked. In her

luxuriant hair was a spray of golden leaves.   Long white gloves added extra elegance. Knowing that large amounts of priceless heavy jewels would be on display, Bella had chosen just diamond earrings and a narrow diamond bracelet.
Her matchless décolletage was unadorned.

She was totally, totally superb, and I knew the huge impact she would make when she sang. A careful kiss, so as not to disturb a single splendid part of her macquillage and she took my arm as we moved off to the ballroom entrance. There we would welcome our guests with Ma and Pa. Ma was her usual unobstrusive best, but the necklace and headband she wore would speak for themselves.

Everyone seemed to arrive together and we were engulfed in handshakes and many good wishes and congratulations. The ladies inspected Arabella closely, for although they may have seen her on stage, they would not have received the full impact of her beauty and charisma.

The gilt chairs were soon all occupied around the floor, and the small tables housed flutes of the finest champagne, as the waiters moved around replenishing the glasses. The orchestra had been playing quietly in the background but now as I judged all to be ready, I gave the conductor a nod and they moved up to full volume.

As I took Bella into my arms and stepped out into the first dance we were open to full scrutiny. Bella had warned me that she felt a little anxious and to keep the dance simple. This I did and with both poise and musicality we got away with it. There was a round of applause, then the guests joined in to display their gowns and jewels.

Ma had surpassed herself with the buffet, which was so fabulous that when supper was announced, it received a round of applause before everyone moved in to demolish it.

Bella had chosen to sing after the plates and glasses had been removed, for she did not welcome distractions. New drinks would be served afterwards for the toasts.
There was no announcement.

Bella merely stood alongside the piano and kind of commanded the ballroom into silence. With total composure she launched into the first of her three chosen pieces. Because of its great popularity in America she began with a downcast 'Butterfly', next because she was even now studying for 'Carmen', the tempo increased, and she became a torrid Spanish cigarette girl, all allure and sensuality. This was conveyed entirely by her gestures, staccato movements and flashing eyes. She would be a sensation in the part.

Finally she had chosen a love song from Show Boat. As she reached its final lines – 'Might as well make believe I love you. For to tell the truth – I do!'

My fine baritone voice joined in. As I stepped forward, Bella was so surprised that only her experience allowed her to reach her soaring top note. With hands clasped, we bowed to our guests and shared a lingering kiss.

I am sure there was no doubt in anyone's mind that this was a true love match.
'Lovely' and 'Well done' rang out as the waiters produced new glasses of champagne, whisky sour or wine.

Pa proposed the couple's very good health after paying generous compliments to his new daughter- in -law.

I replied thanking my parents for an unforgettable evening, and the company for their very generous gifts.
Sean took the chance to whisper to Bella 'Brilliant my dear!'   I could see that she noticed him eyeing up some of the flamboyant jewelry on display, but merely smiled to herself.
Surely he wouldn't dare!

At the approach of midnight the orchestra leader asked for the floor to cleared. Two columns formed down the length of the ballroom and hand in hand, we passed between them waving and calling ' Goodnight'.
AND SO TO BED

The next day Bellla and I decided to take a stroll in Dorothea's rose garden.   It would surely have gladdened or saddened Finch as it was at least four times larger than Courtneys.   The fragrance was intense as Bella linked her arm in mine as we walked the paths.

Taking a seat I looked searchingly at Arabella and said
'Why didn't you tell me that Uncle Sean is your father?'
There was a lengthy silence
'No one ever spoke of my father.   When I asked for him my mother told me that he was away.   I was used to the footmen and the gardeners.   On Sundays there was Mr Goss and Mr Levett to play the organ and to teach me to sing, so I stopped looking and waiting for my father to come home.'
'One day when I was 5 – my 5th birthday in fact, Ivy the nursery maid told me that it was my father, Sean O'Donnell, who had painted the big wall in the nursery before I was born.   She showed me his name and the date.   But Ivy where is my father for he never comes to see Mother and me, and it upsets me?'

'Oh sweet girl, he was lost at sea so he never will come to see you.'

'So I had no father, and just got on with school and singing.   I had Mother and Aunt Alice and Lady Cynthia and Caro and Richard when he was home.   They say that what you don't have you don't miss but I missed having a father sorely.'
Bella paused, a little overwhelmed I think by past memories.

'When I visited FAIRHAVEN during my tour and met you again I was so surprised but tried not to show it.   Sean was charming, welcoming and full of Irish blarney. Suddenly I saw myself reflected back to me. No one else seemed to notice anything amiss. It was when he invited me into the picture gallery that we quickly had a moment to admit our recognition, I from the name on the mural, and he from our looks and my description of Courtneys.'

'We must never let your Aunt guess that their marriage is bigamous, since my Mother must have been alive at the time.' 'Darling Francis, will you take me to visit his gallery and leave us to talk and decide what it is best to do? How did Penelope come to meet him when he had been 'Lost at Sea?'

'Oh he arrived here to open a gallery selling mainly Irish portraits and sporting prints. It was an immediate success and he had a ready supply from his homeland. He could paint himself – quite expertly. With his good looks and charm he was the 'available bachelor' at many a dinner party.'

'When my Mother and her sisters visited the gallery he escorted them and somehow gravitated towards Aunt Penny, as they had been seated together at a recent dinner. Penny was a widow, and she and Sean decided to marry after a short courtship.' 'The families all live together here at Fairhaven in their separate apartments. Uncle Sean is a very popular addition to the family and to local society.'

'So now you know that your ultra charming, popular Father, my Uncle by marriage, is an ultra plausible BIGAMIST. He really must have cursed his luck when you appeared. Now with your marriage to his nephew his whole comfortable life could come

160

crashing down. Pa has made sure that Ma and her two sisters are independently wealthy. Even if his gallery doesn't make a dollar of profit, he is sitting pretty.'

'We all like him, I like him! Who could have guessed his background? I'll do some checking up on his past businesses. Suppose that he moves around opening up wherever there is a wealthy family? Talk about opportunistic, but maybe it was pure chance. What will you ask him?'

Arabella was unsure of her answer, but she must formulate some pertinent questions. Dare she ask if he had bigamously married her Mother? She had always felt protected by his name on the marriage certificate and her birth certificate. Did she really need her few illusions shattered? Perhaps he would lead the conversation.

I had one other thought to share before we went in. Both my Mother and Sean were seen as great conversationalists. They couldn't be more opposite while Sean was never lost for words Ma is fairly quiet. She smiles and asks questions. As soon as that is answered she asks another. So it continues, and her circle is convinced that Ma is quite the greatest, cleverest woman of earth because she has listened intensively to them! Clever Ma!

'You must decide which role you wish to assume. Come my love, coffee and an early bed beckon. Tomorrow who knows?'

The next day – for tomorrow never comes – we arrived at the Antrim Gallery for Bella to keep her midday viewing appointment. As agreed I left her there before Sean appeared.

Arabella after perfunctorally inspecting some very respectable portraits, entered his office.

'So Arabella – pretty name for a pretty girl - where do we start? Please first tell me your date of birth. ' This done he said 'Yes, your conception fits between my marriage to your Mother and then my moving on to Scotland. You have my looks and that slight reservation of Evelyn's, which made her so attractive to me.

Where your wonderful voice comes from, I'm not sure, but the Irish have ever been minstrels and entertainers. I am inordinately proud of your great success even if I cannot claim you.'

'Will you please stop Sean for I find myself unable to call you father. I think you must tell Penelope that the news of your first wife's death was wrong, and that she has only recently died. This makes her marriage to you illegal, which sounds better than bigamous. If she really cares for you she will swallow the lie. Then you should take a long holiday. Back to Ireland perhaps to buy more stock. Marry there very quietly and legally this time. I shall be often at Courtneys or on tour, so we need not meet frequently. Do you think that we can behave as before – civilly and even affectionately? You have done me a great wrong by allowing me to believe that you were dead. It has been a huge shock to find you alive and thriving in a very fortunate milieu. All the ladies may forgive you should you decide to tell the family, but Mr Grantley will be less easily convinced. You must decide, and tell me which path you intend to take.'
Having delivered her speech calmly Arabella, was amazed when her Father embraced her and kissed her on the forehead.

Although he then rather spoiled the effect by intoning 'Bless you', in the manner of a priest.   Despite herself Arabella laughed, so did Sean, and in that way they established some accord and went out for coffee together.   The decision was up to him

The days passed happily and too lazily.   Francis was back into the office every day and was always home very late.   Left to amuse herself Arabella took long walks and helped Dorothea in the garden.

Not only did she diligently do her vocal exercises she began to learn the role of Carmen fully.   She had thought of inviting 'Fitz' to help, but knew by the strange feeling of being incomplete, that she must soon leave.

Francis was needed in the business, and would find it difficult to understand her need to leave him and return to Courtneys.   They would miss each other desperately but it must be so, and would probably remain so, moving between two continents throughout their marriage.   He knew the irresistible pull which Courtneys exerted on her.   Indeed he had felt it himself when he was tutor there and must accept it.   Wherever he was he carried the Hoppner portrait with him and hung it in the bedroom.
'This is what our children will look like Bella',
but, as she smiled back at him she held a great fear hidden.

She was due to see a very eminent gynecologist in New York while waiting for her boat to England.   Then she would know for certain if she could bear a child or was infertile.   Grave fears assailed her for they had been married for months and had been intimate many times before.   Neither had her two previous short relationships, of which Francis was hopefully unaware, resulted in a child, unwelcome as that would have been. Bella could only wait, worry and hide her concerns.

America was a great and wondrous country and a fine place to live, but how she longed for the smallness and stillness and familiarity of England.

The five ladies of the family accompanied Francis and Bella to New York for an evening at the Metropolitan Opera, now one of the most pre-eminent opera houses in the world. The great Nellie Melba was appearing and Arabella gloried in the performance. It was a fitting finale to their honeymoon and they spent the night in the fondest of embraces, he in a kind of rapture to absorb the very essence of his beloved wife.

Bella's secret appointment was quickly and discreetly kept. Francis saw her and Maire aboard with a very considerable amount of luggage and waved until the great boat was out of sight. Dejectedly he turned away. Business and power might fill his days – but oh the nights!

It was raining heavily when Arabella and Maire returned to Courtneys. They both ran for the door, which was flung open by an excited Bridie. All was chatter and bustle as Arabella went down to greet cook and her two loyal maids.

They all seemed well, and Bella retired to the library and left them to learn all about life with a hugely rich American family from Maire. Bella sank into a chair with a sigh of relief. How lovely not to be on show to Francis's family and friends. To be scrutinized when on stage or in her professional role was normal for her, but the environs of FAIRHEAVEN was more difficult. Now she realised how Francis must feel when he was at Courtneys, though on a much smaller scale of course. She had got on really well with the family and so admired the Fairhaven paintings.

Enjoying the tea and toast which Bridie brought for her and which was still her comfort food of choice, she promised to tour the house tomorrow and to catch up with all the decisions which awaited her. For now it was enough to absorb the lovely aroma of books. Her thoughts turned to Sir Edward and his great kindness and generosity to her. How strange to think that had she not cleaned out the library for him she would not have received the wonderful Audubon bequest only to find that it had been cannibalized by Richard.

Without that she would not be sitting here now, the Chatelaine of Courtneys, and responsible for a great house and estate.

How aware she was of all the men and women who were making

it all possible for her, and what a huge help to have a Courtneys account and personal allowance from Francis.

What a wonderful event the reception for her and Francis had been, and who would have guessed that he had such a a powerful and tuneful voice. What a surprising husband he was. Perhaps he should sing a duet with Finch at the tenants' and staff hog roast. She would put it to him!

Bridie had made sure that there was a fire and the customary rose on her desk. Noticing the pile of waiting letters, Bella knew that her responsibilities as owner of Courtneys would soon crowd in upon her.

Arabella wanted to visit her Aunt Alice at the cottage. Evelyn had willed it to her sister in recognition of all the help that lady had given in raising and advising Bella.

She must catch up properly with Cook and Edie and Millie. Bridie would have a deal to tell her. Then there was Mike Roberts and the Irish brothers. Bella had brought gifts for all of them all chosen with American influences.

For Finch and Maggie Jones she had chosen two large Stetsons and could hardly wait to hear Finch's loud 'YAHOO', which she knew would erupt.

Bridie raised her from the sleep, which she had fallen into. The fire was burning brightly, and a table was laid before it. Dropping off for a few minutes had turned into two hours, and she felt refreshed. Quickly washing and changing into her Courtneys uniform of plain skirt, white blouse with a wide belt she descended for her supper.   Cook had excelled herself producing a meal from Finch's delicious produce.   A light soup was followed by chicken and a cornucopia of vegetables.   Cook's special fruit jelly with thick cream and luscious grapes with slices of English cheeses had never tasted so good.   To know that it was produce from her own garden and the farms on the estate made such a difference.

Normally she would have invited Bridie to join her for coffee.   She knew that the two sisters' reunion would be Irish and voluble! There was always the morrow.

The pile of letters and packages was too inviting for any woman to resist, so she worked her way through them steadily.   Some were to be enjoyed, some invitations to be evaded, and those relating to her career from Hugh and her agent were of particular interest. John Jarvis had forwarded information and figures prior to their meeting for her information.   There was much to be considered so an early bed was indicated.

Out of habit Bella ensured that the fire was safe to leave.   The Audubon book was a great treat to save and savour in the days to follow.   Those days became constantly busy.   It was all she could do to find time for her essential vocal excercises.   Yet it was also a time which brought her much pleasure too as she re-connected with Courtneys and the rhythm of its life, and of all those who served it.   They were its life blood and with their help Courtneys would stand proud as it had done in good times and bad.

Beautiful, classical, comfortable again and still exerting its magic on those who shared its trials and its glories.

First came Bridie as house manager. She had no major worries, and felt that the staff were coping well. The work had been manageable because Bella had kept her word and there had been no entertaining which involved big dinners and guests staying overnight. Should that happen they would need to refurbish the remaining five bedrooms. Some new linens and kitchen equipment for the newly ambitious cook were needed.

Since Bella had left for America Mike Roberts had concentrated his efforts on the outside areas. The laundry had been equipped with the 8th wonder of the world – an electric washing machine. This and the electric carpet cleaners were by far the favourite pieces of equipment, saving hours of heavy work. The laundry maid who Bridie had brought in for two days a week to reduce the work of Edie and Millie, was at first suspicious and then thrilled. Also new were men's and women's W.Cs with access from the outside only.

Then it was the turn of cook who was still in a daze of excitement with her new sink and cookers and refrigerator. She wanted for nothing except those items which she had listed for Bridie.

Mike Roberts followed. The meeting took the form of a walk around the house and outbuildings. He had taken advantage of her absence to complete the nursery – at Francis's request.

With sadness clouding her pleasure – for she was still not pregnant – she applauded his improvements. Her Father's mural looked fresher against the newly decorated and relit walls. A new nanny would find every modern convenience, and both her and her nursery maid's room sunny yellow and cheerful. The new laundry room, storage areas, W.Cs and stable accommodation were so well designed and well fitted. It was no wonder that the Noonan boys and Micky, the stable boy, had never moved out. There was now only the trap pony, for when Francis was here he hired a horse or borrowed one from Christopher. However there were now two motors. Liam had learned to drive and was now house chauffeur while Micky was on 'general duties '. This mainly meant assisting and annoying Finch.

Arabella now moved to what was to be a very enjoyable meeting. Archibald Finch was by now 68. He had always looked the same, but now seemed a little more stooped and wrinkled. His eyes still held a twinkle and he still called her 'Miss Arabella', and always would. Bella greeted Maggie Jones, and then Mr Finch escorted her around his domain.

 'It's grand weather Miss Arabella but it will soon turn now. It's not been a bad season and ah've got some good apples, pears and root veg in store. The grapes ave been specially good when I can keep them thieving birds out 'o me greenhouses. And that thieving Micky off me apples'.

Finch looked pleased when she admired the last of the roses, which he now favoured after his success with 'Lovely Evelyn'!

'Fancy her saying that 'is were as good as them at that posh American place where Mr Francis lived! An' theirs were four times bigger too. Well good luck to 'em. All that prunin' an' feedin' and dead 'eadin'. Archibald Finch didn't envy 'em one bit.

Then Miss Arabella dropped it on'im. Mr Francis wanted to sing a duet wi' im at the ox roast. He was to let 'er 'ave a list of suitable songs to send to Mr. Francis. Good golly an' 'im nearly 70. Just shows what a special singer 'e must be. That 'ud cost the lads down at The Fox a few pints'.

'The Morris dancers, would go first an' get 'em a bit merry fust so's they all gets tangled up. Jed wi' 'is accordion, Nat on the fiddle 'an Josh on the squeeze box. Wi' them boys an' plenty o' barrels of ale everybody 'ud 'ave a great time – an' if they could remember it they'd not drunk enough.

And I'd wear me Stetson!

And shout YIPPEE!

John Jarvis had a longer list with farm rents and tenancies to review. Arabella asked him where they could hold the ox roast and bonfire. With all the estate, the cottages and the house staff there would be too many for Courtneys. Had he a farm with a big enough barn and a willing farmer to arrange it all. He thought that Alec and Mary Foster would agree to do it.

'Please do ask them Mr Jarvis. I won't see them out of pocket and it will be of such assistance as I am so busy now with rehearsals in London. Also please invite them to a meeting on Tuesday evening. I thought that if we all met up with ideas, we could agree and settle matters. Then everyone would know what the others were doing!

The meeting was held in the library after an early staff supper. As requested everyone had their ideas list and fairly whizzed through the agenda, which Bridie chaired very efficiently. No-one messes with Bridie when she's on the warpath.

Items agreed were:-

Date   Friday week

Venue   Mr and Mrs Foster's big barn

Remove excess straw bales and use rest for seating

Side tables to be set up.

The landlord from The Fox and Hounds to supply drinks and be in charge and the Irish boys to help serve.

Micky and his pals to set and light bonfire.

Butcher Banks and Farmer Roberts and their team to supply, roast and serve the ox.

'And could it be young and tender please' piped up cook.

Butcher Banks to control carving and portions

'Very big please.'

Mrs. Foster to work with cook to arrange various dishes from the farmers' wives.

Edie, Millie and Maire to keep an eye on the children and stop them falling into the fire pit.

Bridie to keep an eye on everything – Especially Mike Roberts no doubt.

Finch to be sure that the Morris Men were ready for their spot – He would certainly be ready for his with Mr Francis.

The band to play merry music for lots of country dancing.

John Jarvis as estate manager, was to propose the toast to the new Mr and Mrs Grantley in beer and cider on behalf of the company.

It was set to be the liveliest night that anyone could remember and all would recall happily for years. The meeting retired to the kitchen for sausage and bacon cobs with loads of mustard and beer and tea to lubricate their throats.

Francis arrived on the Wednesday before and managed to disappear into Finch's bothy on several occasions.

All was expectation and excitement.

Arabella awoke with a smile of contentment. Her reunions with Francis were always exciting and sometimes exhausting. He made love to her with such controlled fervour, that she knew that he was hoping that this time she would conceive.

His father must be expressing concern that they should not leave it much longer. How could Francis explain that it was not for the want of trying? Bella felt sad concern for her husband. He must hang the John Hoppner of the two beautiful children in that bedroom with such hope only to be regularly disappointed.

No time today for gloomy thoughts for this was to be a day for celebration. She and Alice had considered whether out of Evelyn's memory they should hold the ox roast. Alice was strongly of the opinion that their tenants and the villagers wished to show their respects for the couple who ran the estate with so much thought for all the people who lived and worked there. Things were so much better for everyone since first Arabella and then when Francis had taken over, and they were grateful.

Also the chance to celebrate a wedding, have a bit of fun, and quite a bit to eat and drink, was not to be sneezed at! The clincher was that Evelyn would most certainly have wished them to go ahead.

Francis went up to the site with Mike Roberts to check that all that was needed was in place.   He reported back to Bella over lunch, Maggie Jones had quietly decided to decorate the barn with bunches of Autumn berries, drying lavender and golden daisy chrysanthemums.   It had brought the whole place to life, and with bowls of red apples looked lovely.

Maggie had proved to be an inspired choice by Finch.   Bella had noticed that she could and did turn her hand to any jobs that needed doing.   Maggie was the person turned to by the stables, the kitchen, the builders for first aid, and even by Bridie if she had an insoluble problem.   Always calm and level headed, she inspired confidence rather in the way that Evelyn had done when she was Courtneys' housekeeper.

Arabella really hoped that no Sean-type suitor would breeze in and sweep her off her feet for she was the natural successor to Finch.

Nothing could have prepared Francis for the scene that met their eyes when he and Arabella entered the Foster's barn. He was used to the rather staid functions of his parents and their friends.

Here was all noise and colour. The bonfire blazed and crackled outside the open side of the barn. The smell of delicious beef roasting pervaded the air. The tables groaned with every kind of rustic food. The ale kegs were lined up behind the table already bearing four barrels, with Paddy, Liam and Mr. Hallam and Albert from The Fox cheerfully on duty. All of them were sporting red and white striped aprons as they pulled pints and half pints for a demanding crowd of cheerful revelers.

The accordionist and fiddler were playing merry tunes, and folk were either singing along or dancing.

Francis and Arabella had arranged to arrive after the food had been served so as not to inhibit the guests. They need not have worried. Apart from waves and shouts of greeting, everyone just got on with their grub. So did Francis and Arabella finding it extremely good. Butcher Banks and Farmer Roberts carving arms were growing weary as the feeding frenzy was dying down.

Archie Finch called up the Morris dancers before they 'bust' with food and drink. It was as he had guessed. They started off in good order, but liberal libations of beer got them and the waffling of the waffle sticks became a bit haphazard. Percy shouted at Pete to keep in time but all ended in good humour and harmony. So it continued until everyone had finished. Plates were cleared and glasses recharged.

Then with a flourish of the accordion up stepped the surprise item and sensation of the night! Old Archie Finch with Master Francis. To everyone's astonishment their voices blended in spirited renditions of well-known songs. Bowing to demand they gave an encore. Finch waved his Stetson in acknowledgement, shook hands with Francis and the accordionist, sat down and smiled and smiled with satisfaction.
YES OLD FINCHIE SMILED!

John Jarvis proposed the health and future happiness of Mr. and Mrs. Grantley, which was supped with enthusiasm.

Francis replied in his cute American accent, thanking everyone for their kindness and welcome to a foreigner come to marry their local girl. He loved both her and Courtneys very dearly, and hoped for very many years with them all!

Their applause was replaced with Oh's and Ah's of surprise as with loud bangs and fizzes, dozens of fireworks exploded from beyond the bonfire. The effect of the glowing pyramid of flame with so many rockets and shooting stars and showers in all colours was magical.

The children forgot to be tired, and thumbs in mouths watched in awe.

It was such a wonderfully fitting end to the night and shouts of thanks and delight left the happy couple in no doubt as to the happiness and enjoyment of everyone there.

Did Arabella imagine it, or was there a special glow to Courtneys that night. As Francis and Bella looked up at the stars Bella remembered her mother saying:-

'When your parents die, there is no-one between you and the stars.'

She fixed her eyes on one star and bade her Mother 'Goodnight'. To her father she gave no thought at all.

Christmas 1908 and New Year were spent at Courtneys for Francis wanted to be in England for Arabella's opening in Carmen at the Coliseum.

The season was to be quite short running for only six weeks. It was a critical success, though it did not always play to full houses as the weather was so wintry.

Arabella was contracted to Hugh to tour the opera down America's east coast. This would allow her to sail over with Francis and join him at Fairhaven when she had completed her tour. This she would do with much relief. She still felt uncomfortable in the role that was so different from her calm English rose character. She had been well rehearsed, and taken classes in Spanish dance to enhance her performance. 'Butterfly' might have been an odd role for her, but all was sad acceptance. 'Carmen' had to be strongly acted, and while she was up to the challenge she nevertheless did not inhabit the part of such a fiery and sensual woman who could captivate any man. Neither did she now enjoy playing in opera.

When you gave a recital all was on your own head, and to some extent that of your accompanist. In opera much depended on fellow cast members, a duet had to be balanced with a tenor. Any one could be 'off' at any time and reduce the cohesion of the entire performance.

1909 passed in the usual transatlantic see-saw and she did not tell Francis of her decision to revert back or retire until Christmas. If only she could become pregnant, then the decision would be made for her.

There 1909 Christmas was spent happily enough at Fairhaven with Francis's family welcoming her in their usual warm- hearted way. Their immense wealth gave them such assurance that they were never uncomfortable in any situation.

Arabella found herself very uncertain on the times when she was required to spend time with her Father. Sean had managed to whisper 'Not Yet' in answer
to her raised eyebrow. So Penelope was still a 'bigamous' wife, with no idea of the fact.

Christmas was splendid and celebrated in huge style, with many guests to lunch and dinner. Bella had told Dorothea that her voice was very strained after touring such a demanding role. That kind lady let it be known that Bella was rather exhausted, so not to press her to sing. This occasioned many speculative glances at her midriff, which caused her to flush with embarrassment and further inflame the rumours.

They returned to London in the New Year with Bella desperate to return to Courtneys, and to her friends there. She noticed that Francis seemed to have more and more business meetings. When she asked him where he rather defensively said, 'Oh, Government offices. Quite boring really, but very necessary for an international company like Grantley Industries.'

Exactly what offices she wondered? It was when she dropped him off in Whitehall and her cab was held up that she saw him enter the War Office.

Randolph had made no attempt to hide from her and Dorothea that the Company fully expected war with Germany. Not soon, but soon enough.

German ambition for control of the seas, and to expand its empire would put it on a collision course with the rest of Europe. Whatever Congress might say about isolationism, America was sure to be drawn in.

With that in mind the Grantley Corporation was investing in more steel works and clothing factories, for uniforms would be required. Randolph kept tabs formally through the company and informally through Annette and Phillipa on

the aircraft and motor industries. Their tentacles spread ever further for Randolph had thrown his not inconsiderable weight behind the research and development into what he thought would win the war on land – the tank.
So far progress was very slow, and the result too heavy and cumbersome.
He was not discouraged, for hadn't he built a business on hunches?

So now Francis was meeting with British officials to talk of armaments and supplies for the expected future war.

It was discovering this secret, which made Arabella decide to act on one of her own. One October day when Francis was once again in London, her morning post contained a letter from America. Taking it to the small sitting room, Bella lit the kindling already laid, for it was a cool morning.

The letter held news from the consultant in New York, which was unexpected. He begged to inform her that the results of his tests and examinations brought him to the conclusion that she was not infertile. She was ovulating normally, and could conceive a child at any time. The relief was overwhelming, the conclusion and realization earth shattering. If she was fertile then Francis was not! How could she tell her beloved husband such devastating news? News, which must shatter his self esteem, and thwart his family's plans for a future successor. Bella immediately cast the letter and envelope into the flames, for no-one must ever know or guess its contents.

Suppose that she suggested to Francis that they both consult a specialist in London for some help. A little subterfuge, but at least they would both be investigated, and yes she could bear to go through the tests again. Yet when the results came through Francis would still be faced with their unbearable reality. No – not yet, she still needed to work this out somehow.

One further secret could not be kept and was set to explode. Mike Roberts should have his name set in the stone of Courtneys, and in the house archives for his outstanding work. He had overseen and organized all the changes, which had improved the house so completely. He had now been 'Clerk in charge buildings' as we called him for several years. Everyone thought of him as being as permanent as the house itself. When he stayed on to help John Jarvis with upgrading the farms and cottages, they became even more convinced of his permanency. Everyone knew that Bridie had a 'tendresse' for him, and no one resisted Bridie. When he came into the Library after asking to speak to Bella she believed that he wished to tell her of their engagement.

Instead he dropped the bombshell, that it was time for him to return home!

Like Francis he thought there was to be war in Europe and he preferred to be in America. Would Arabella be prepared to waiver his notice and allow him to leave at once? There was a suitable boat sailing. He did not wish to have the farewell dinner offered him – just to say a general 'Goodbye', shake hands all round and go. His fiancée was getting restless and wanted him home!

HIS FIANCEE - whoever knew about that? Bridie's hopes would be shattered! Neither could Arabella believe that he wanted to leave so precipitously. There had to be a reason.

Three months later when Bridie appeared a little red-eyed but somehow triumphant I knew the reason.

'When did this happen?' Bella asked.

'Oh Miss Arabella' she said slipping into her old form of addressing her.

'I've loved him to bits for ages. When he told me that he was off back to America and without me, I couldn't bear it. I just slipped into his bed one night and let nature take its course. Then he was ashamed and couldn't wait to go, and we all thinking the world of him and nobody wanting him to leave. I'm glad of this child, and I'll tell no-one who the father is, though folk will gossip and put two and two together.'

Bella thanked Bridie for confiding in her, and said she'd think what was best to do. She knew that Bella would never turn her way. She'd got Marie and it would be like Evelyn and Alice again.

Bella whispered to herself – ' I don't think I need any more secrets.'

I had told Hugh of my plans to retire. He was quite understanding and had not pressed me to change my mind, so it was with some surprise that I received a letter asking me to reconsider. Puccini, whose music suited my voice best I think, had written a new opera called GIRL OF THE GOLDEN WEST. It might just have been written for me.

Its heroine was a feisty American girl who rode and shot like a man, and was confident and free spirited. It was all action and not your typical opera story at all. Since I neither rode nor shot, it might be difficult to get into character. With Francis's help I would be able to achieve a credible American accent.

So into rehearsal I went and at once knew that this role would suit me completely. I didn't just act and sing the part of MINNIE – I was that girl.

Bob Jackson was a dynamic producer and enthused the cast and crew. My 30th birthday was spent in a rehearsal room, but that is what is likely to happen in the world of music.

We were to sail to New York for two final weeks of rehearsal prior to our grand opening at the Boston Opera House. It was a huge investment for Hugh, and I was determined to be at my best to repay his faith in me.

The newspapers were already featuring tit-bits of gossip about the opera and its 'socialite' leading lady. I might have supported both charity and society events with the Grantley family but I was by no means a socialite.

It was strange that no newspaper had featured my 'Rags to Riches' story. Surely the rise from housemaid to international singer, to wealthy industrialist's wife, would have made stirring copy. Imagine the headline! – CINDERELLA STORY OF GRANTLEY WIFE'. May we be spared that!

Another item, which must never be aired, was a simple single sheet of paper in a letter with a Dublin postmark. It read – 'All Done' and was initialed S & P.

So Penelope was now my step-mother and Sean's legal wife. I destroyed the letter immediately and thought of my Mother instead.

We opened 'Girl of the Golden West' to sell out audiences. The Gala opening stopped traffic, with people gathering to see the clothes and jewels of the elite audience. For them the opera was sung in Italian. For less fashionable audiences we sang in English. This suited me, and my ebullient character and the rugged tenor was American. 'Triumph' is a word I do not use lightly, but so Girl of the Golden West turned out to be. Soloists and ensemble were as one and the whole performance was full of vitality. It was an unusual subject for Puccini to have chosen, and was to be a failure in Europe initially. How clever of Hugh to realize that the subject would be irresistible to Americans. With opera I found the strain on my voice and body was intense. My fitness had never been in doubt, or more demanding. For three years I had been a housemaid and there is no finer exercise than running up and down flight after flight of stairs for up to sixteen hours a day.

That is not to mention a succession of physically demanding jobs. Even so a tour must be carefully planned with rest periods in between engagements.

I spent several of these at Fairhaven with Francis and his family. I wanted above all to study the pictures in the long gallery. Francis was brilliant at describing the significance of so many details, which I had seen but not really understood before.

A boy would usually be shown with a dog, a girl with flowers or a pet bird. Books on a pedestal indicated learning and a woman cradling a child with an older one nestling into her skirts indicated that she was a mother to several children. Sir Joshua Reynolds was never a favourite of mine, but his study of Sarah Siddons was masterful.

We resumed our sketching, and he became my tutor again. This meant that I relaxed more rather than ranging over the countryside, and so was well prepared for my next engagement.

It also meant that I spent a lot of time avoiding my Father who seemed determined to make up for all the lost years. I think that I was pleasant enough, but in a subtle way by my slight coolness indicated that his Irish charm and wit were rather wasted on me.

The company always had several days of re-rehearsal both technical and musical before out next opening. Hugh insisted on this and Robert Jameson fully agreed. An unprepared company could never give of its best.

At our final performance we encored so often that Bob had to step forward to give his 'FINALE' speech. We drank champagne on stage, bade each other farewell, packed our traps and went our separate ways. Maire was well prepared for us to make a quick getaway, so we avoided the too long and too theatrical 'Goodbyes'.

No one but Hugh, my agent and Francis knew that I had just given my final operatic performance. Francis was waiting at our hotel. He presented Maire with a golden locket with a fine diamond in its centre. Frank Lewis was to take her out to dinner at an exclusive restaurant.   All I wanted Francis and I to do was to have supper together in our suite. I wore my simple 'Courtneys' uniform. Happily my skirt was green satin and my belt of softest blue leather.

The food trolley had arrived, and Francis was to serve us. On my plate was a jewellers box. It contained the most sensational emerald and diamond ring. The stones were dazzling, and I was duly dazzled and amazed at Francis's devotion. By the time I had thanked him the meal had to be re-ordered.

Wasting no time we sailed for England as soon as possible. Our crossings were such a regular part of our lives that it was easy to overlook the comfort and luxury of our suite. I was a good international traveller, but once at Courtneys developed a severe aversion to leaving it.

Sea air really is good for you and we arrived at Southampton feeling fresh and invigorated.

As expected, Francis and Frank Lewis left us in London, while

Maire and I continued to Courtneys. Would I ever tire of the sight of my beloved home? As it came into view my heart leapt. As I leaned my head onto its warm stones I felt courage and peace and hope flow into me, and thanked my God for Courtneys.

As ever Bridie was first to greet me and Maire. The months of our absence had seen a great change in her for her pregnancy was well advanced by now.

I asked her to join me for tea in the library, where so many decisions had taken place, to make one more. First I needed to know what Bridie's own wishes were – Ireland or Courtneys or somewhere else entirely. Without benefit of marriage there would still be a stigma among some people on the estate. Her accent seemed even more pronounced, but if I expected her to be contrite I was much mistaken. She needed this child to remind her of the wasted years while she waited for Mike Roberts to declare himself. Fool that she was! Now she must look to the future for herself and her child.

Both Paddy and Liam Noonan had offered to marry her. When each of them 'wanted to make an honest woman of her' they soon left with a flea in their ear! Like my Mother before her, she wanted to return to work at Courtneys. She had thought to perhaps engage a nursemaid for her son – for so she had decided that her child should be. When I at once offered her the use of the nursery she declined.

'Sure it's like this Miss Arabella. I don't want him brought up at the top of the house alone. I want him to be out in his pram watching the world go by. Then learning to toddle and walk around the garden and the stables and to climb trees and find bird's eggs and all the things that lads should learn. There'll always be one of us to keep and eye on him. If he tumbles down he'll learn to jump up. Young Mickie'll have him on the pony's back before he can walk. Old Finchie'll be cursing him for scrumping apples and strawberries before you know it. If we can live in two of the stable apartments it'll be fine, and I'll not let him interfere wi' me work here.'

Her impassioned speech reminded me of how I wanted my hoped for child to grow up, free and adventurous. Perhaps they would grow up together, like Richard and Caro and I had done.

So it was all arranged. Bridie's pregnancy had not always been easy. I insisted that she take some leave to prepare for her confinement. Her layette was in place; sewn like mine 30 years before, by Aunt Alice. What a trouper that lady is.

Like my Mother, both facing childbirth without a husband, Bridie longed for her son to be born. Unlike my Mother his birth went smoothly assisted by Marie. Dr Daniels was well pleased with mother and son, and flattered that Bridie immediately named him Eddy, after the doctor.

Eddy looked entirely like his bright-eyed smiling Irish Mother, with not a sign of his quiet fair-haired father. His dark hair would soon grow and curl like Bridie's and Marie's. Never did a child have so many willing slaves. No prince ever received more love and attention. In short, he was just the sort of child that Arabella longed for and she loved him dearly.

Would she herself ever know the joys of motherhood?   How long must she wait?

Chapter 52   Archibald Finch   1910-1911

Why do them city folk reckon that nowt ever 'appens in the country? Well it jolly well does 'ere at Courtneys! In fact it niver seems to stop 'appenin. Damn good job ah've kept fit all me life. Ah puts it down to niver 'avin married, damned 'ard work in all weather, an' a pint or two an' a yarn down at the Fox's most nights.

We was all right glad to 'ave the Missus back from America, wi' Mr Francis to follow soon. Ah've 'ad a lot o' years 'ere, an' grand years they've bin wi' Sir Charles an' Lady Cynthia. Then Miss Arabella – dang it, I'll niver call 'er Mrs Francis – takin' over when Richard gambled it all away.   Ah've seen about thirty winters an' summers since ah' got the job as 'ead gardener. Ah were a bit young fer't job, but Lady Cynthia didn't know the proper plant names and ah did!

That time when, back in 1908 Miss Arabella cum to see me an Maggie and' gi' us the Stetson 'ats, ah couldn't help tryin' mine on an' a' shoutin' YAHOO just like them cowboys do in the pictures. O'course yer can't 'ere 'em, but the words cum up on the screen an' yer can see their mouths movin'. It wer' great an' when Miss Arabella told me ter look out me songs. I never dreamed as Mr Francis 'ud want to sing a duet wi' me. I'll look em out tonight an get'em to 'er so she can let Mr Francis know. Then like I told 'er, I'll get them Morris dancers goin' an' the fiddlers revved up.

Well the ox roast were brilliant though ah couldn't remember too much about it after we'd sung. We'd got two songs worked up, but then 'ad to find an encore. Down at the Old Bull an' Bush did

190

well enough.   Ah thought then that ah'd give up singin' after that cos nowt'll ever beat the ox roast.   Then them fireworks as Mr Frances ordered frit the kids to death.   But that were all two years ago now.

Then summat did beat it!   We all knew as' that cheeky minx Bridie 'ad 'er eyes on Mike Roberts for years an I betted that Maire weren't far be'ind.   He'd oft time cum into the Bothy an' share a cup o' tea wi' Maggie an'me; an' al'd noticed 'er givin' 'im one or two long looks an' all.   Anyway in 'e comes, shook 'ands wi' us both an upped and left.   Just like that!   Me an' Maggie were flabbergasted and thought as' ow summat were up. Summat were up alright.   Up the spout!   Bridie were goin' to be left oldin' the baby right enough.   She'll not marry either o' them Noonan chaps which'll put their Irish snub roses right out o' joint. Can't say as ah blames 'er.   They'd soon be throwin' it in 'er face when she cum to give 'em their orders.

Any road why are they still 'ere?   They cum wi' the builders an' niver went.   Suppose they do 'ave their uses wi' the boiler an now the 'lectric generator an all.   That Paddy patrols at night wi' 'is great big club and Liam 'elps wi' any job.   He's supposed to be great wi' the hosses but we all knows 'as ow it's Mickie who does most o' the work.   Now Liam does the motors and gits to wear a fancy uniform 'cos Mr Francis paid fer im to learn all about motors.

Any road whoever knew as Mike Roberts 'ad a lass waitin fer 'im in America.   She musta' bin a patient sort.   Ah miss 'avin a yarn wi' 'im an' a game o' dominoes down at the Fox.   Now we've got a kiddie.   Bet as 'e'll turn out to scrump me best apples!

Arabella afterwards wondered whether the seeds of that day had been sown at Richard's 21st birthday ox roast. When they met in the barn-dance it was only too obvious as was his partiality towards her which could not be mistaken even by an innocent seventeen year old.

Then there had been his theft of the Audubons, where he had lost face, and finally her purchase of Courtneys, which must have been a bitter blow to him. Now with her wealthy marriage, she owned the entire estate. They say that money and power are great aphrodisiacs, yet surely hatred, desire and frustration must be their equal.

Taking her daily walk often led Bella to the forest glade where she had spent so many magical days of her childhood. To see it recaptured in the nursery mural had added to its enchantment. She was deep in happy thought when the soft whinny of a horse alerted her to the fact that she was not alone.

She saw Raven before his rider emerged from behind a tree. He had obviously been drinking, with the high colour and tousled look, which she still remembered from their meeting in the library at Courtneys, which had ended so badly. She had hated him that day and despised what he had become. In his turn, self-loathing could easily be turned and blamed on her.

After years of sobriety, he had started to drink again and knowing of her return from America, this had enflamed him. Today Richard could resist his pent up desires no longer. He had spied on her for days and had laid his plans carefully.

'Don't be afraid Bella I just needed to speak to you ' he reassured her disarmingly. Yet when he was close enough, he sprang at her. With an arm around her shoulders and a hand clasped over her mouth he swept her off her feet and on to his riding cloak spread out on the grass and well hidden by bushes.

Neither did he tear at her clothing but just methodically removed her blouse and underwear. Bella did not scream or cry out. His intensity terrified her into submission, for she saw that there would be no reprieve. Richard seized her mouth with a rain of kisses, and then launched his assault on her.

How he had longed to possess her luscious body, how he had need of the intimacy of such closeness. How sweet was her subtle perfume, how full and firm her breasts. He had dreamed of these moments for so many years and tried to blot her out with alcohol and other women. Might as well compare a perfect rose to a dandelion. He was determined to reach the heart of the rose, and to pluck its petals on the way. His every plunge into her softness brought him nearer to his purpose.

He looked down into her violet eyes, which had beguiled him and haunted him in equal measure. Now they stared at him in hurt despair. Could Richard really be so base? He covered those eyes with his hand for he knew in his bones that their distress would haunt him. He wanted her look of love and desire – not this.

Still his need carried him on, for he surely knew that this would be his only chance, and its memory in every pulsating detail must last him for the remainder of his days. The heat and demands of him seemed to Bella to go on forever. He whispered her name, yet shouted his demands for she had withdrawn before his main assault in both thought and spirit.

Richard wanted that spirited girl he had seen at the barn dance, not this submissive silent creature. He redoubled his thrusting efforts. At last Arabella lifted her body to his as his irresistible stimulus overtook her. Her blood surged and sang in her ears as she drew in great gasps of air. Her silence was broken by moans of pleasure, and his searching tongue met hers.

He made love to her as he rode to hounds, reckless, inspired, with great leaps and slower troughs, swift short burst then long low lunges. He must remember every moment as petal by petal he opened her centre and with one final thrust and a great cry of triumph he emptied his seed as high up inside her as it was possible to reach.

Then he stretched out alongside her, and laid his head on her breast. He realised that his insane assault had at last turned into an expression of his love.

Both of them knew that this must forever lie hidden from the world, and both of them knew that in the final moment they conceived a child, who would carry on the genes of the Courtneys.

At length he lifted her up and helped her to dress. A little crumpled perhaps, but no torn garments to reveal her total ravishment.
'If you meet anyone say that you have fallen', and he smeared her cheek with soil. Then he took her by the shoulders and kissed her

on her forehead.   Mounting Raven he bowed to her from the waist, saluted her, said one word 'Arabella', and rode away.

Bella walked slowly back to Courtneys and reached her bedroom. She bathed, dressed her hair and made her face up carefully.

When Francis returned from London on the following day she greeted him with a loving smile, a tasty supper and an alluring dress.

She knew that she must ensure their intimacy immediately.   That way she would never really know who had fathered her child.

As the weeks passed Arabella found that she could begin to blot out Richard's assault, but never her shameful response to it. After three months she consulted Dr. Daniels who confirmed the happy fact that he was at last with child.

When she told Francis by cable of her news his joy was unconfined.

Randolph was ecstatic that their great family industrial corporation would at last have an heir. For Sean it was a grandchild, which he could never acknowledge.

At home she told only Alice and Bridie for she was now thirty-one years old, and feared to announce her pregnancy too soon in case of a miscarriage. Bella need not have worried, for like her mother she had a relatively easy time. Her only concern was that Francis was once again tied up in America. The tentacles of the Grantley Corporation were becoming ever more far-reaching. It had invested in so many industries, which would expand during a war. Randolph, like all the great industrialists before him, saw the prospect of war as a business opportunity and invested accordingly.

Now Arabella had another concern. Before her pregnancy, Francis had suggested that she might like to visit Germany with him on a business trip. Since she had always disliked and struggled with the German language she had refused his offer. So he went with only his valet.

Francis was due to be away for two or three weeks, but she did not hear from him. Neither did Maire receive a letter or cable from Frank Lewis, whom she had lately taken up with. Francis was usually quite descriptive of his business trips on his return. This time he said nothing and when she questioned him he managed to distract her. Had he answered with only sketchy details she would have been sidetracked. Now she knew that he was misleading her. Bella did not sleep well that night.

Christmas 1911 was so different with a small child in the house and seemed very special. Eddy received so many toys and so much attention. His reaction to all the bustle and sparkle and decorations was to chuckle and reach out for everything to put in his mouth.

Bridie's plan to live in the stable accommodation had worked out well. Eddy's pram could be out of doors on fine days, and in the housekeeper's room or kitchen on cold days. A wooden spoon and a saucepan lid made great and simple toys and a tin of dried peas a rattle. The possibilities were endless and cook and the maids were both inventive and attentive.

The 'Kitchen Christmas' as they called it was its usual success with gifts and goodies from Fortnum and Mason hampers well received as ever. They were the only sign of Francis, for he was now required in Washington by the American Government and would travel to England for his child's birth. Alice was struggling with poor eyesight, so Bridie and Maire made some of the layette and it was easy to buy from the big stores.

Sometimes Arabella just sat daydreaming about the forthcoming birth of her child. Just as it had been violently conceived would its birth be so?

After her vocal exercises each day Arabella had taken to reading some of the books with which Francis had restocked the library. She saw that much of her later education had resulted from travel and art. Now she tended to read some science, history and illustrated works on nature. Each day she turned a page of the great Audubon book and studied his technique, which helped her to improve when she sketched herself. Bella was entirely content and only ever walked in the garden now.

Spring burst forth in all its new life, and the wonderment never left her.

Courtneys seemed to spring into life as the gardens burst into
flower with all the spring bulbs and shrubs.   Finch was the first to
rather grudgingly admit that Maggie had made a huge
contribution.   She never seemed to tire and now that Mike and
Mr. Francis had given them two new lads, bulb planting in the
gardens and naturalizing daffodils in the park had made this year's
show spectacular.   Arabella was fond of snowdrops so there were
banks of these near to the house.

And among them all romped that cheeky minx Bridie's cheeky lad.
If Bridie had spirit then Eddy had more and in spades, and the
household had a job to keep an eye on him.

When Mickie took him out to look at a horse and foal on one of
the farms, Eddie made for the lambs and started to frisk and play
with them.   Their mothers were too astonished at this two legged
lamb to chase him away!

Like all large houses Courtneys had its share of infestation.   That
word covered insects, bugs, birds and rats and mice.   Constant
checks were made for wasp nests, birds in chimneys and gulleys.
A swarm of flies usually indicated a dead beast somewhere.   The
drains were kept flushed and disinfected.
Mike Roberts had left 'CHECK BOARDS' for every season, and
these were strictly adhered to.   He left the pursuit of moths in
carpets, curtains, wardrobes and soft furnishings to Bridie and the
maids.

Against rats and mice Courtneys had a lethal answer.   This had started as a cross between a corgi and a Jack Russell. The result was a killing machine. Ginger in colour with a pointed muzzle, short coat and tail. Their offspring had sharp eyes, which missed nothing and sharper teeth, which could snap a rat's back in a flash. This was matched by a turn of speed and change of direction, which was astonishing. They considered themselves always to be on duty, patrolling

Finch's gardens and sheds, and the house from top to bottom, on search and destroy missions. Bridie was especially watchful in winter and spring. Best of all were the stables where they lived and the barns, which were their natural killing grounds. Their progeny had been spread to the estate farms so that Courtneys estate was far less ravaged by vermin.

A litter whelped and when they were able to be released into the wider world, Eddy was taken to see them. In his rush across the stable yard he fell quite heavily, tripping on a raised cobble. Before he could start to bawl and Maire or his best friend Mickie pick him up, a furry small animal darted to his side and began to lick his face and give funny little barks. So there it was, he had a nursemaid, companion, playmate and guard, all in the shape of one small dog.

He christened her Flossie, and she was the only dog to be allowed to stay in the house for Arabella rather disliked dogs. They played together for hours, chasing balls, throwing sticks, looking for rabbit burrows, and all the other things which concern small boys and small dogs. Flossie's sharp teeth would grab at his jersey and pull him back if she thought that he was being too bold. If he was in trouble she barked her head off to summon help. It was a great relief to Bridie.

Arabella was by now six months pregnant and after some whispering and covert looks at her midriff had told the staff that she expected a child in the summer. She told them over morning drinks in the kitchen. It was here that they still met for important decisions, which involved them all. She insisted that they each have two weeks holiday so as to return refreshed. She answered all of their questions willingly. It was agreed that this year all spring cleaning be completed early, and holidays taken before the end of May or after August.

Bella accepted their exclamations of delight and congratulations. Here were the people whom she was closest to. Here they had hatched their plans for

Courtneys and worked like troopers to clear out all the rubbish, dirt and neglect. They had carried on when she needed to leave them to earn more money. They had withstood the dirt and chaos caused by the builders, and no doubt had a few sweethearts among them! Yet none had left her or Courtneys. Cook was already widowed and 'Didn't want another bloke, not no how never.' Bridie had fallen for the wrong man, and Maire loved the travelling life and looked to America. She had determined to ask Francis if there might be a place for her at Fairhaven? Edie and Millie and been with her since 1907, and with homes in the village were likely to settle on village lads for husbands. As her mother had predicted they had turned out to be strong and faithful.

All of them loved nothing better than to share a cup of tea

together as she told them of the great cities where she had sung, and the famous people she had met. Now they would expect and accept that her touring days were over. Whenever she returned from her travels she made sure that Maire bought gifts for them all, for were they not the backbone of Courtneys?

Bella asked Maire to tell the 'Irish lads' as they were still collectively called, and set out to do the same for Maggie and Finch. How Francis would take Maire's request for a transfer to Fairhaven she was unsure. He had been devastated by Mike Roberts' betrayal of Bridie until she had told him that it was Bridie who had instigated the final act. Also Mike had worked tirelessly at Courtneys and was still much valued at Fairhaven. After an initial uncomfortable meeting, they were back to their usual good relationship. Did Mike ever think of Bridie she wondered?

For herself, she tried not to think of Richard, or to remember their encounter in the glade. Yet what woman experiencing their growing stomach and bosoms would not? She was now at her womanly best, for being with child agreed with her.

She forswore any form of corset, and wore the same style of skirt and blouse adjusted to her new dimensions and the season. 'Peachy' could best describe her complexion, and her eyes shone with health and happiness. This contentment was marred by the frequent absence of Francis and her worry as to his whereabouts and what he was doing. American citizens were not subject to the suspicion showed to the English abroad. Very wealthy Americans and their interest and promised investment were very welcome indeed.
The Germans proudly showed off the great efficiency of their

factories and furnaces.

As she sat in the library one evening with a book idly on her lap, Arabella again thanked Sir Edward with all her heart for this sanctuary. Arabella prayed that her husband with his quick wits and charm would return safely to her. She longed for him and for the birth of their daughter – for she knew that the child she was carrying would be a girl – in some way a replacement for Evelyn.

When Miss Arabella came to see Maggie 'n me, Maggie carried behind ' er a try o' hot tea an' Irish cake.

We sat in a sunny corner o' the garden away from the breeze. There weren't a gret' lot to see.   Just the over wintered broad beans an kale an' all the stakes showin' where the early seeds we' set.

When she quietly told us as ow she were expecting ah couldn't 'elp jumpin' up gi'in a YIPPEE even tho' ah were only wearin' me old cap.   Maggie an' me were plain glad for 'er and Mr Francis. They'd bin married for night on four years, an it were gone time there was an heir to the place.   These gret big 'ouses need the family al' all its' istory to keep 'em goin'.   The ah remembers as'ow it were Mr Richard as were the Courtney.   Not to worry, Miss Arabella 'as loved Courtneys since she were a toddler.   Now she were goin' to 'ave a lad to tek it over.

Gret news and gret cake and all.   That Bridie 'ad bin a bit 'eavy on the whiskey, an' no mistake, an' all the better fer it.

It'll be like the old days an' Eddy an the new bebi can play together. I'll wait fer it to cum an then ah'm goin'n to retire; an leave everythin' to Maggie.   Ah've already given 'er the lads to train an' when ah leaves I'm goin to give 'er me journals.   Ah'll keep the songs out of the back of it – just in case like!

My Father is a powerful man and has insisted with the Government that I do not return to Germany. I am grateful because on my last trip I felt that I was under suspicion and that my credibility was wearing thin.

Grantley Corporation had extracted information, and I had asked the questions to which the military needed answers. Yet the promised investment and information on our tank research had not materialized, so perhaps they were becoming impatient or I had let down my guard and been too obvious in posing the questions.
Clumsy of me.

When I had given every scrap of information in Washington, I returned to Fairhaven to see the family. They were all concerned. This would never do as Arabella expected me back fit and well and must not suspect what I had really being doing. Frank Lewis had not been idle either, for he had kept his eyes open and noted the civilian situation. There was a war like feeling among the citizens. Everyone was on edge as if waiting for the first shot which would trigger a war. He did not write to Maire, nor I to Bella, so there was no visible connection between us and Courtneys.

I missed America, I missed its mood of optimism can-do and almost light heartedness, for Germany seemed – well – Germanic. I had no doubt that war would come and that they would be brave, determined and well equipped enemies.

As soon as I could I needed to sail for England, good old dependable England, with its certainties, its class distinctions and good manners on one hand, then Finch and Bridie and the Irish boys on the other. It felt safe in the security and power of its huge Empire. I knew that they would all fight but with greater armaments and the U-boats they would have a stiff task ahead.

Now I must put all this behind me and concentrate on my wife and the longed for child which she was carrying. We had been apart for too long, and just when she needed me most. Now I intended to stay close and America and Grantley Industries must survive without me, for my wife needed me more.

Once the strain of being constantly on my guard lifted, I began to feel and look better. My Mother ensured that I had the best care, which was formidable. Early bed, warm and cold baths, constant warm and cold drinks, small but nutritious meals, and best of all the time to relax and let the strain drain away. The family had to wait for me to approach them and not to badger me into conversation – especially not to question me on Germany and my views on a likely war.

Although I protested, I secretly enjoyed Ma's attention and felt able to face the voyage. They sent me on my way with gifts for Bella and the baby and with so many good wishes. I could not help noticing that Sean seemed a little uncomfortable, but he gave me the most wonderful drawing of a child for Arabella.

Frank Lewis had been a rock of support to me and had also had a complete break from duties, for there was more than enough staff at Fairhaven for someone to take over as my valet.

During the voyage I may have been unsociable, but I really needed to rehearse what I must say to Bella.   During my last German trip I had realised my vulnerability.   Should I have met with an 'accident' she would have been left a widow with a tiny baby.   I had of course made very adequate financial provision for them both, so that she could remain at Courtneys and afford its upkeep in the future.

However here I am safe and well and concerned that we never spend so much time apart again.   It had been hard enough being separated during her tours, but I was now 42, and wanted us to be together constantly.   That word resonated with me for we were constant to each other, and I longed to be with her throughout the coming years.

We must decide where we were to make our permanent home.   I knew that her love for Courtneys was all encompassing, and that she hated to leave there.   I had thought that she would miss performing, but as long as she kept up her vocal exercises she seemed content. So content that I feared that she would immediately reject my offer of a new home in America one that would be separate from Fairhaven.   We could establish our own home on a much smaller scale, more manageable and more private than the large family at the Haven.

To say I feared her answer was an understatement.   My Father still took the major responsibility for a huge and growing conglomerate.   He showed no sign of slowing down – in fact he appeared to thrive on the work and on making the many decisions required daily.   Nevertheless he was 67 and needed me there regularly, not for a few months each year.

I had a duty to him and the business and a duty to my wife and child. 'Whither thou goes I will go' was biblical but still a truism. I expected Bella to agree to join me in America as soon as our child was old enough to travel.

It had become our habit to meet in London, when I returned. Being on 'neutral' territory allowed us to re-acquaint ourselves for a few days. We visited the great galleries, attended the theatre and dined together in some luxury. We returned to the Savoy or Claridges or Bella's favourite The Ritz. Here Bella could enjoy the piano expertly played as we dined or took afternoon tea. Our re-unions were wonderful, and we were seldom recognised. On each of these occasions I prevailed on Bella to choose a piece of jewellery as a token of our
renewed love. She disliked ostentatious jewels preferring a simple strand of pearls or a necklace and bracelet of filigree gold of fine workmanship.

I had given her Cartier or Bulgari on several occasions. This time because of her advancing pregnancy I was to travel directly to Courtneys. As I looked for a suitable gift I saw the most perfectly matched necklace of glowing amber. I knew that this would wonderfully offset her violet eyes and golden hair.

We met as we always did with like minds, and the love, which sustained us when we were apart expressed in every form. Love and laughter at her new rather swollen stomach when I had to stand back a little and reach a little further round to embrace her.

The staff all greeted me warmly, and then discreetly withdrew. I had been away too long. We walked as we always did in the rose garden and sat in the 'iced cake' summerhouse to just look at each other.   I drank in her beauty, which seemed to me to be enhanced by her pregnancy and the joy that it brought her.

It was quite impossible to express my own feelings.   We had waited so long for a child, been disappointed so many times, and now all seemed set fair.   Bella asked me if I had any preferences for our little one's name.

'No darling, it really is your right to choose! If you should bear a son I would rather like his names to include Randolph, and you?' Bella had obviously considered the matter at some length for she instantly replied.

'JOHN JAMES RANDOLPH GRANTLEY'.

'Why so sure' I asked

'Because of JOHN JAMES AUDUBON and the huge part he has played in my life here.'

'And for a daughter?' I asked

'I'm still unsure, though Dorothea for your mother and Evelyn for mine, will appear.'

I handed her the box containing my gift, and as we looked at the necklace we said together –

'Of Course – AMBER'.

So a daughter was to be called

AMBER AUREOLE DOROTHEA EVELYN GRANTLEY

Bridie came to tell us that supper would be ready in 30 minutes if we wanted to change.   So we dined simply in the library and toasted Sir Edward in champagne as we always did.

As dusk deepened so did our need for each other, and we retired to bed.

As I hung the Hoppner painting of the two children over our bed, I did so with a full heart knowing that at last our family was to be. It was only when I met Eddy the next day, that I saw that he could have been the model for the merry-eyed curly haired boy in the painting. As he frolicked with his small dog, I knew for a certainty that our child would be the girl with the daisy chains.

It occurred to us that the staff had all been with Bella since she had bought Coutneys in 1907, and Bridie as her dresser. Why in all the years had not one of them left or married, for five years is a long time? When I discussed it with Bridie she explained the reasons.

'We were good and considerate employers. We paid good wages, on time. Arabella had always done so from the beginning and because of her background and experience we shared in any problems and asked for their opinions. We shared meals and ideas. We respected them,'

However it seems that Maire wants to work in America and both Edie and Millie's sweethearts were getting restless. They were waiting for our child to be born, and when Arabella had recovered, they would give notice.

Changes afoot all round.

AMBER AUREOLE DOROTHEA EVELYN GRANTLEY was born on a fine late July afternoon. Her birth had been both protracted and difficult. Arabella's labour had begun on the previous day.

Francis and Christopher Richards had become good friends, bonding over their love of automobiles. Both enthusiasts and knowledgeable on the workings of the combustion engine they spent considerable time together exploring its mysteries.

Christopher tended to drive a little too fast and was completely surprised when his motor veered off the road at a bend and crashed into a high stone wall. It was only when he tried to move that he realised that his leg was broken. His extreme agony told him that. Taken by ambulance to the County Hospital he slipped into unconsciousness. When he emerged it was to see a serious handsome woman in full charge of a team of nurses who were tending to him. His leg had been set and immobilized for some time. When he had at last regained mobility – albeit with a pronounced limp, he had returned home to introduce Laura Stanley as his wife. They had quietly married by special license to avoid the fuss due to the heir of a wealthy, though not noble, family.

Laura and Arabella had liked each other at their first meeting. Bella admired Laura's calm common sense approach to any situation. Laura admired Bella's determination to buy and restore Courtneys before Francis came to the rescue, as Bella told her how she had forged her career to fund the acquisition and rescue.

That day she and Christopher had motored over for coffee when Bella's waters broke. The men were quickly dispatched to find Bridie and fetch Edmund Daniels. Laura and Bridie got Bella to her room and Dr. Daniels arrived. It was really the three of them that saved her life and that of her child as the fight to deliver her began.

Conceived in a fury of passion and violence, the baby it seemed was determined to stay in her cosy nest. The prospect of emerging into an uncertain world did not appeal, and she fought against Arabella's attempts to deliver her. When Bella was exhausted and had, like Queen Victoria, been given chloroform to ease her distress, then at last Amber appeared red and angry and squalling! Bella's three carers had only taken short breaks and were exhausted too..

The noise brought Francis and Christopher running to be reassured by the Doctor that all was now well, but the new mother needed a little time before Francis could go in. Both men and the Doctor needed a little restorative brandy. Francis decided that childbirth was not for the faint hearted.

Amber thrived but her Mother was slow to recover from the birth. The nursery was hastily transferred down to two large family bedrooms so that Mother and baby could be close by. Bella slowly began to walk between the two, then downstairs for the first time, then at last into the rose garden and summerhouse.

Her daughter spent time outside in her pram. When she could sit up Eddy and Flossie were never far away. Amber had not inherited her Mother's violet eyes and blond hair. Her deep blue eyes and titian hair made her striking in a different way.

Christmas 1912 was to be the last small intimate one in the kitchen. Edie, Millie and Maire would be leaving in the New Year. They enjoyed every minute of it and the Irish lads were in fine voice and on fine form. Finch and Francis left them to it and Bella had not sung in public for many months.

After Christmas Francis's family were due to visit Courtneys at last. Francis spent the time that he was not with Arabella supervising the bedrooms and agreeing with Bridie on their guest allocation. All was in hand and extra staff had been interviewed for the invasion of nine American guests. Only Uncle Sean had sent his apologies. Bella could not stifle a wry smile.

It was intended that the two new maids would be retained for when Edie and Millie left at last. Francis and Bella had no intention of trying to emulate the butler, footmen and myriad staff at Fairhaven.

Cook would have a full time assistant, and an extra kitchen maid. Bridie, Maire, Edie and Millie were fully experienced and would ensure that the new staff in their new uniforms would be equally efficient.

Bridie was quite excited by her new responsibilities and happy to see that the staff quarters would at last be fully occupied. She hoped that the visiting ladies' maids and valets would find England 'quaint'. She had thought of promoting the Irish lads to footmen, and then remembering their fondness for the drinks they would be serving decided perhaps not.

213

Mr. Francis had ensured that the cellars were well stocked and had employed a sommelier who knew his job to ensure that the drinks would be properly chambre'd or chilled, the spirits and cordials always on hand and that Randolph's favourite beer was in stock.

With Christopher and Laura and his parents as guests together with Lady Cynthia and Caroline the dining room was set up, and a 'trial dinner' given.   With the usual assistance of those extra helpers, Mr. Fortnum and Mr. Mason, all went well.   Any glitches were noted and would, hopefully, be corrected.

Francis and Bella had determined that a warm welcome and the beauty and comfort of Courtneys would compensate for any lack of grandeur.

The winter of 1912-13 was unusually kind and when the Grantley family arrived at Courtneys in late March with much blowing of horns and cries of 'Welcome' the weather was mild and sunny.

As you may imagine the reunions were enthusiastic and both Courtneys and Amber were greatly admired.   Mealtimes were noisy and expansive.   Outings were got up to visit nearby places of interest.   Francis's intrepid sisters were lent horses by Christopher, and took to hunting, having read so much of English hunting traditions.

The men were happy to shoot and their expertise ensured that the Grantleys were on every hostess's lists.   Randolph and Francis went up to London for several meetings and returned tight lipped.

Many after dinner frames of billiards were played and may cigars smoked. It was all extremely convivial.

The ladies discussed not fashion and staff but the Suffragist movement, which was becoming ever more militant, and aeroplane – and – car – engineering and design. They brought with them the ideas of mass production lines and their efficiency in the face of increasing demand. The fear of an evermore militant Germany and the discussion of the likelihood of war was not just a male prerogative.

Bella and Laura came to admire these feisty American women. It was only the liquid tones of Bella as she again sang after dinner, with Sean's wife Penelope proving a more than capable accompanist, which interrupted their talks.

Dorothea devoted her time to amber spending as much time in the nursery or wheeling the child round in her splendid perambulator as possible. The month
was speeding by and the spring bulbs were again beginning to light up the gardens.

As for Randolph, who had thought that the days at Courtneys would be endless, he came to understand what 'timeless' meant. Habit saw him rise at his usual time, but breakfast was not the usual hasty meal taken before he was driven to the station. Here he breakfasted in a leisurely manner and enjoyed the English breakfast enormously. The staff learned that repeated cups of coffee were required to keep this larger-than-life American fueled. He took the newspapers and more coffee to the little summerhouse and took in the world news. Courtneys seemed so small and confining after Fairhaven, yet so delightful and comfortable too.

He knew he would not see Dorothea until late morning, until she had seen Amber safely settled in her pram. Dorothea had insisted that he carry a pen and small notepad with him at all times. She knew that his agile mind would still turn to business matters. If he jotted his ideas down it would assist him when it was time to cable his head office. Only regular contact with his business had kept Randolph away for so long, that and Dorothea's determination to remain with Amber and Arabella for the intended time.

Francis had still not spoken to Bella about their future. He was due to return to America with Randolph and the family for three months.

It was in fact Dorothea who broached the subject.
'My dear Bella, Francis would never have married unless it was to you. Neither did he ask you to stop touring or limiting your career. I know that he has helped you enormously in your determination to restore Courtneys. I know how much you both love it here and now I understand why.'
'But my dear he <u>must</u> be in America Francis has huge responsibilities with the Corporation. I know that it is his fondest wish for you to establish your own home near enough to New York for him to come home to you both each evening.
To deprive him of his wife and child is so cruel, I see the hurt in his eyes when we sit down to dinner at Fairhaven and he always alone. Francis needs you my dear and I do urge you to join him. It would be intolerable for you both to find yourselves separated

216

by the Atlantic Ocean should war break out.'

Arabella listened attentively. She knew that this was very much on both their minds and needed to be addressed – perhaps when Francis returned in the summer for Amber's birthday? Could she put off the decision until then?

Bella knew that she could trust Dorothea and Francis to find them a suitable and splendid house. She would be charged with making it into a home for them. Could any home equal Courtneys – never! Could she risk her marriage by refusing to join her husband? Grantleys Corporation was such a huge and important company. Surely that made it even more important than Courtneys and the estate.

Whichever way she viewed the problem the answer was obvious. She must return to America with Francis, Amber and Nanny after Amber's first birthday in July. Bella had made her marriage vows, and must abide by them.

How, she wondered, could she divide her heart between Francis and Courtneys?

Arabella and Francis always seemed to have their most important conversations in the library or the little summerhouse. She did not leave it until his final day but spoke to him on the same evening.

'Dear Francis – I realize that I cannot bear to let you go – and yet I must. We seem so complete with Amber and now you must leave again. Our marriage seems to be becoming more separate, and it's too cruel on us all. When you come back for Amber's first birthday I want us to return to America with you. I know how vital your work there is. If you can find us a house – modern and not too big – that would be wonderful. I'll just bring Nanny and employ American staff. They may find my English ways strange we'll soon get used to each other, and your Mother and Aunts will help me.'

His look of sheer relief and happiness made Bella feel guilty, but she continued.
'There will need to be some changes here before we leave. We may need to close Courtneys down and just retain caretaker staff. What do you think?'

' That might be best, but don't cut too many. We don't want to come back and find everything in disrepair. I'd keep Maggie and two boys for the garden, the three Noonan boys for heavy work, security, the pony and one motor. Then the boiler and generator need Paddy. Then Bridie and two new maids, one of whom can cook! It really is your decision Bella.'

Randolph was now into his new routine. When Amber was settled he and Dorothea strolled around the gardens together. Then they enjoyed a light luncheon with whoever was around. Next he nipped into the summerhouse while Dorothea read. She played with Amber and soon enough, afternoon tea was served on the terrace if the weather was kind. He particularly enjoyed Bridie's Irish whiskey cake!

One afternoon he was woken from his nap by some very fruity language. There was an old gardener trying to tie up a rambling rose branch, which was just out of reach and sprang back each time he captured it.

'Dang blasted awkerd b………, come 'ere!'

'I'll give you hand,' said Randolph.

By the time they had wrestled the recalcitrant branch into submission and Finch had secured it, an unlikely alliance had been formed.   It was them against a wall of thorny roses.   Randolph was a little snagged and the odd thorn had speared him.   Yet suddenly he felt really relaxed and happy.

Finch led him to the kitchen where Bridie quickly bathed his scratches with salt and water, and supplied them with mugs of tea. TEA!! They took them and Maggie's mug with Irish cake as a special treat down to the bothy.   English-accord grew, and from then on Randolph was given a job each day, and rewarded with TEA and cake.   When he'd met the |English garden lads and the Irish lads, he knew that when war with Germany came, no-one would defeat these chaps.

For Luke and Simon every day at Courtneys saw them gaining new skills too.   With their wives out hunting or visiting with new friends on non-hunting days,

they were left to their own devices.   This meant long days of training when they were not out shooting.

They were in so many teams back home that every day was training day when they were not at the Grantley offices. Deprived of their rowing and sailing, they decided to run.

Armed with a map of the area, they explored.   Gosh, it didn't look far to anywhere, until they realised that all the paths and roads were narrow and winding. They often took the wrong way and arrived at the village or farm they were aiming for either hot and sweaty or wet and cold. And that didn't allow for the folks they met on the way.

There was always a damaged cart wheel, or a car that needed a push, or a load that could do with a hand from a couple of strapping Americans. There was often a farm kitchen and a cup of tea, TEA! and cake. When they made it to a village pub there was warm beer and fat cheese and onion cobs and darts. Never ones to resist a challenge, they were repeatedly beaten until Francis found them a board and they practiced every night after dinner while Francis, his Uncle Steven and Randolph played billiards. America had showed 'em at the 1908 Olympics and America must show them again in the Limekiln. Britain were never going to win the America's Cup back because Luke and Simon would be on the American team.

Meanwhile Penelope, who was missing Sean, and Hilary and Simon were driven to all the historic places of interest in the area. They returned glowing and full
of the interesting facts they had learned about wonderful furniture, pictures, silver, porcelain and the gardens on view. It didn't seem to matter to these families how dilapidated their houses were becoming, they just lived as their ancestors had done seemingly uncaring of the worsening situation in Europe.

As he prepared to leave, Francis had reminded Bella to have the annual inspection and to repair any problems.
'Also do make sure the staff look out for infestations. I'd hate to

find wasps nests and ants everywhere. The dogs must go in regularly too. Look at Mike Robert's check list and add to it. We'll go over it together when I return and I'll do the same with Steve Maitland – the new Estate Manager.'

Arabella had enjoyed her American family's visit, and was delighted with their praises of Courtneys and its staff. They were all real characters but hard working and efficient.

They left with many expressions of gratitude and had enjoyed their visit hugely and had made many new friends. They were to spend two days at the Savoy to look over London where Francis would join them later for journey to Southampton and the boat home.

Amber waved to them cheerfully from her pram.

The staff had lined up either side of the door in the traditional manner. Bella took her husband's arm and smilingly walked back in. The Americans had been fun and popular with everyone. To Bridie's surprise each of them had shaken hands with the line up, and Bella knew that big money had been left with Bridie to be handed out. Randolph had already given Finch a goodly sum, for one of his tasks had been to visit the 'Fox' inn. Over an extended lunch break they had drunk warm beer and met Finch's pals. Randolph bought drinks all round, then Finch followed suit. My these Brits could drink. He'd have to have a lie down when he got back. Finch's standing had never been higher!
When Dorothea had kissed Arabella goodbye meaningful looks passed between them. Dorothea could hardly bear to part with Amber who small as she was knew a devoted slave when she saw

one.

Timeless had not been timeless after all thought Randolph as they drove away. The Company had not gone bust and his daily cables had dwindled to VERY URGENT ONLY.

My master has started to drink again.   It will be the same as when he lost Courtneys.

That is a day that I will never forget.   He usually hunted three days a week with a second horse each day.   On Fridays he rode CAESAR, while I ate and rested before the Saturday steeplechase. He was in an especially good mood on steeplechase day, and I heard him laughing with his friends as they laid their wagers for there were new riders who were rich and wagered heavily.

On this particular Friday Caesar was lame so I was saddled as first mount and Star was due to replace me as second horse.   The new groom waited at the wrong place, so I had to hunt on in heavy ground.   My master knew that he should stop but a fox was sighted, the 'TALLY HO' rang out and off we ran.   I was very tired as we hacked back and the stable lad was told to feed me and tend me carefully but I was still rather stiff and sore the next day.

The wagers had been huge, for when Master Richard had been drinking, he threw caution to the winds.   When I saw a new chestnut that I had not raced against before I knew it would be a close call.   So it proved to be.   Normally I would just have beaten him but with my stamina sapped by the hunt, he caught me and passed me a furlong before the finishing line.

I hung my head in exhaustion and despair.   My master had never carried a whip for our mutual understanding saw us through. Now I felt a terrific blow on my neck as he struck me with his fist. There was a loud murmur of disapproval from the spectators.   I knew that he had not meant it, but had been carried away with his losses and what they meant.

He immediately stroked my muzzle and begged me to forgive him, but we still had to leave Courtneys to settle his debts.
I was going to miss Micky and Old Finch and the apples and I never did forget Old Finch and his cursing, and those wonderful fragrant apples.

The next years were hard and sometimes exciting. We had no settled home except when we stayed with Lady Cynthia, who had forgiven her son. So we became 'Rovers' riding all over in all weathers. We stayed at cheap inns where the ostlers were often careless. Sometimes I was left badly groomed and ill-fed.

My master was little better; but when he received his estate legacy, he stopped drinking, bought FOX HOLLIES where the house and stables were both comfortable and we settled down happily.

It all changed the day he met Miss Arabella in the woodland clearing.

When he rode off in triumph it was as if we had won the greatest steeplechase ever. Then his moods began to swing between glee and self-loathing.

When Miss Amber was born and the news reached Fox Hollies he became very quiet.

We still hunted regularly, but I was as regularly rested, and the grooms were careful and kind. Often there were two lively fearless young American ladies out with us. They had to be reminded by the Master to give the hounds room.

One day my master ordered me to be saddled, and as he mounted I heard him mutter the name Amber. We headed towards Courtneys. It was time for a special apple or a juicy carrot!

With utter suddenness I was down and Master Richard had been flung over my head and lay without moving.

When I managed to stagger to my feet my near foreleg and the hoof, which I had caught in a deep hole were badly damaged. There was no sign that my master was moving. I whinnied and nuzzled him. At last I seized his jacket in my teeth and pulled and pulled until he sat up, groaned and held his head.

We had gone through other falls together and he had always got up and remounted. Now he mumbled and shambled up to his feet holding on to my mane and then the saddle. His 'Get on Raven' made me limp on towards Courtneys, dragging him along, and with my lame leg causing me agony with every step. Two miles seemed like twenty; and as I came nearer I whinnied as loudly as I could.

Surely Micky would hear me and know that it was the sound of a horse in great pain. I heard the blast of a whistle, and, as my master fell to the lawn I took a few more paces to clear him and collapsed also.

It was Micky and Old Finch who saved me, and Maggie Jones and Maire who saved Mr. Richard. I think it was Archie Finch's swearing that did it!

'You dang blasted hoss, what 're yer doin' a rollin' on me lawn? Git up yer blasted thing'. And other words too strong for me to tell.

While he swore at me Micky and the lads cut the girth and pulled the saddle aside so that dry blankets could warm my back. I was given a drink and my leg was bandaged, for Micky was sure it was not broken. I heard him say
'We've got to get him up Finchy or he'll not make it.'

The thought of not having me to swear at livened old Finch up no end. He knelt at the side of me, shook my bridle and then gently stroked my muzzle. Then he said loudly,
'If you git up, hoss, ah'll git up an' all an' ah've got three apples in me coat'.

Then he heaved himself up and offered me one of those luscious apples – but he held it too far away for me to reach.
'Git up Raven, git up lad.'
This was the only time he had ever used my name. I'd always been 'That danged hoss' or 'That black devil'. So now I just had to get up. It took me a while and I got my apple with another held out tantilising in front of me. I sort of hopped to my old stable. There were extra layers of soft bedding to cushion my hoof and leg and some warm mash with chopped up apples and carrots.

Mr Appleton the vet came to check me over, and Micky never left me.

'It's the worst sprain I've ever seen, but no breaks and no damage to the frog. Keep him warm and give as much water and small feeds as he wants. I'll look in tomorrow, Micky.'

His instructions were carried out to the letter, but Micky and the Irish boys had a secret weapon, and took turns to use it. I was massaged with warm oils and a little embrocation for my legs. This released my sprained muscles, and I began to recover. It helped that old Finch visited me daily. He hung over my stable door and called me a 'Daft great hoss'.   He thought I didn't notice when he gave me an ordinary apple not a 'Garden of Eden' I did, but we just looked at each other and he grinned at me.

No one ever mentioned Master Richard. I only ever saw him once more and I never left Courtneys and Micky and old Finch again.

My glory days might be over but I had enjoyed such times of excitement and Master Richard would never be forgotten. A bond is a bond and ours was unbreakable.

When the whistle blew we all ran outside. It was a signal, which had been arranged by Mike Roberts, after a builder had fallen and lay undiscovered for far too long.   One was kept in the kitchen, Bothy and stable to summon help quickly.   When we heard three loud blasts we all ran.

Micky took charge of Raven, and Maggie and I ran to Richard. He was obviously badly hurt. Never had any of us moved so quickly and made such quick decisions. Bridie to get Dr. Daniels, Jean and Stella, the new maids, upstairs to make up a bed and Cook to boil water to bathe his head. Maggie and I scrubbed our hands and put on clean aprons and gathered up what first aid equipment we needed while the Irish boys carried Richard up to the nursery. We had quickly decided with Bridie that this would make the best sickroom, with space, kitchen, bathroom and sleeping accommodation for whoever was on duty. With the staff quarter nearby there would always be someone extra to help at nights.

Maggie directed that we lay a clean sheet over the bedclothes while we cut off Richard's clothes, washed him in very warm water then into a warm nightshirt and into bed.   One of us held his head and neck steady and we worked quickly. The cut on his head was bathed and cleaned as we awaited the Doctor.

During this time Richard barely moved just groaned from time to time and muttered 'Bella'. We looked at teach other but Miss Arabella was out with Amber visiting her Aunt Alice in the village.

The diagnosis was not good. There were no broken bones because he had fallen on soft ground, however his head must have struck something hard. The cut was not large and would heal, but it was the bruising both to the head and the brain that Dr. Daniels feared. He directed us to keep Richard's body lightly warm, but to continuously apply cold compresses to his head. He was to be given sips of water at regular intervals, and chicken broth if he could manage it. His head and neck needed to be kept as immobile as possible.

Maggie devised a sort of wooden clamp lined with soft sheepskin for the purpose. It meant that someone had to sit by him day and night to stop him trying to thresh about. Still unconscious after three days, Dr. Daniels was considering surgeons from London to operate to relieve pressure on the brain. Lady Cynthia and Caroline came every day to sit and talk to him – still no response.

It was only when Miss Bella thought to sing to him, and not a quiet one either but the forceful 'Habanero', that he stirred. Then when she brought up Amber and the child cried loudly at the sight of the sick man, he opened his eyes and smiled.

From that day on he recovered slowly. He could make it to the bathroom though Paddy or Liam still helped him and shaved him. To prevent his muscles wasting one of them massaged him daily with warm olive oil much as they did for his horse. As long as Miss Arabella visited him and read to him as he sat in a chair Richard seemed content. His first unassisted steps were greeted with as much joy as Amber's had been.

Some days he loved to look at the great mural and tell Maire about his childhood. One day he became quite distressed at the sign of it so Maire turned his bed and chair, and placed a screen in front of it.

When Dr. Daniels decided that he was well enough to sit outside it was a red- letter day for all of us who had cared for him. He took coffee with Miss Arabella in the summerhouse. He wished to see Raven, and mark how that brave horse was progressing.

At the end of the week on a beautiful bright day, while Amber sat in her pram and Eddy and Flossie played nearby, Richard said three words –

'I am content'
Then, like his Grandfather before him, he sat back in his chair and died.

Everyone was distraught, for he had seemed so much better. When he visited Raven those two old friends looked into each other's eyes and perhaps, for who knows, said their farewells. As he walked to the summerhouse he had held out his hand to Amber and she had closed her small fist around one of his fingers and laughed up at him.

When Lady Cynthia arrived, her son was laid on the hall table, like his Father and Grandfather with a spray of roses at his feet. She took Arabella into the small sitting room. There she asked that, before she left, all those who had cared for Richard so devotedly gather, so that she could thank them. Then quite firmly and without tears she insisted that her son be immediately removed, either to the Dower House, to Fox Hollies or to St. Bart's. Arabella had done enough – It was time to go.

Courtney left Courtneys on a golden day, so at odds with the man who was leaving it. Perhaps with 'I am content' he had remembered his happy childhood and young manhood before his Father died, and accepted it all.

Lady Cynthia had requested a quiet family funeral, but such was the prestige of the Courtney name that all the staff from the three houses, tenants from the estate and villagers, lined the funeral route from the Dower house to bid 'Farewell' to their former master.

With Richard's accident and death, the final link with my childhood with him and Caroline at Courtneys was severed. I grieved for Richard, preferring to forget his attack and remember happy times. I grieved for the man he could have been – the son and grandson that Sir Charles and Sir Edward had hoped for. All of us at Courtneys had tried so hard to restore him to good health, but his brain injury was too severe.

I comforted myself in that I had forgiven him and that he had been able to see his daughter, however it was the greatest relief to find that when news of his will emerged, he had left everything to Lady Cynthia and Caroline, and made no mention of Amber.

Lady Cynthia and Caroline were dry-eyed at Richard's funeral and in strict control of themselves. I took Caro's hand and held on to her. She looked so terribly fragile that I hoped that some of my strength and energy might flow into her.

There was a small reception at the Dower House as Richard's coffin was taken to the family vault. It lasted only a short time and I was thankful to return to Amber and the certainties of my life at Courtneys.

Caring for Richard had left us short of time for arranging our departure to America and there was a great deal to be done. I had a conference every morning with Bridie, and we both had our lists to work through.

As Francis and I had agreed, the new maids Jean and Stella would remain full time. The three Noonan brothers would still be needed. Edie and Millie had stayed on for the Americans' visit, loyal as ever, but they now wished to marry and move into the village. I did not agree with the custom of making female staff

leave when they married and offered them part-time work or as holiday and sickness relief which softened the blow of their departure.

They were both married from Courtneys in fine style. Cook was able to attend, as the assistant cook could step up. Both were wonderfully happy days, and I gave each of them a substantial monetary gift, which they so richly deserved after working so tirelessly for Courtneys and for me. They were both surprised and delighted.

Maggie Jones and the boys would carry on and the splendid excess produce would go up to Covent Garden. Some small return for the Fortnum and Mason Hampers, which helped cook so much on special occasions. Finch – ever a law unto himself – who seemed to spend most of his time in the stables, would retire when he decided to go.

Maire would come with me as my dresser just for the journey. She had decided not to go to Fairhaven. Dorothea had used her influence and my name to find her a position as Dresser at the New Amsterdam theatre in New York. She would be in the very heart of Theatreland, with all the excitement and celebrities she had enjoyed when I was performing and she was thrilled.

When we added it up there were no real dismissals just Edie,

Millie and the assistant cook to leave by their own choice.

It was only as I breathed a sigh of relief that the hammer blow fell.
Why had I not noticed? Each time Dr. Daniels came it was Bridie
who escorted him and saw him out. Surely and as a widower he
was too old for her? Bridie reminded me that she had been with
me for over ten years. First as my bright eyed, chatty and
efficient dresser and that now, as House Manager, she was in
effect both butler and housekeeper and had been since I first
purchased Courtneys. What a loyal worker and friend she had
become!

She said she was a little tired and a little worried about her future
and Eddy's. The boy was spoiled to death and needed a father.
Who better than the older, wiser and well established local
doctor?

Bridie did not love him in the way that she had adored Mike
Roberts, but she was very fond of him, trusting him to take care of
both her and Eddy. He had a very attractive large home and
surgery in the village, and would make her a dependable, if not
exciting, husband.

At first I did not know what to say. Then I collected myself and
congratulated her warmly with a kiss. But Courtneys without
Bridie – UNTHINKABLE.

This led us on to discussing her wedding, and she will decide what
she and Dr. Daniels would prefer.   It seems that she had thought
of staying with Aunt Alice for a few days, and leaving from there
for a service in the nearest Catholic church. We shall see!

234

Perhaps the break from Courtneys would be too much for even Bridie.

Next with Francis's help I must appoint a new house manager as efficient as Bridie. With our imminent departure to America, it would be hard to train someone up in time.   As we sought for an answer before cabling the news to Francis, Bridie and I looked at each other and both said MAGGIE JONES.
We agreed to await Francis's reply cable, and to meet again tomorrow.

I am finding all these changes overwhelming and Bridie's news is a bitter blow for me.   Already the prospect of leaving Courtneys is unsettling me.   It has been my greatest love for most of my life. How can I bear to leave it?   How will I cope without the reassurance of its golden warmth and comfort?   I had grown up to know each room with its separate feel and ambience, noticed each problem, scrubbed and polished, walked its gardens and sometimes just sat and absorbed all its history.

Then came the unwelcome thought that I had loved Courtneys before I had even met Francis, so which would prove to be more important, and could I balance my emotions?   Amber was missing her grandmother and needed me to spend more time with her, for her little secure world would change too.

Meanwhile I made arrangements for the great Audubon Elephant Folio, and the fine silver, which Francis had bought for the dining room to be moved to the bank in Cheltenham.   The first editions from the library went too and I hoped that Sir Edward understood.   Bridie had set aside a cool, dry storeroom with stout locks for very valuable pictures and other items. We did not wish to denude the house, but must be sensible.

The new house manager must learn the role quickly. If Maggie takes the post, then she must be replaced in the garden. The decisions must be made thick and fast.

Francis was due to arrive any day for Amber's birthday on July 15th, and to stay before we all left for Hartford where we shall make our new home. He had cabled a reply agreeing with our suggestion of appointing Maggie as House Manager. I trust his good sense and experience to see through all the goodbyes and business decisions, and the goodwill payments to the staff for so many years of loyal service.

The surprises for the day were not finished. Bridie invited me with Amber in her pram, and Eddie and Flossie in attendance to visit the paddock nearest to the stables.

Finch was there as usual with Raven looking out over his stable door. There, frolicking in the field was the most beautiful black foal. I am not fond of horses, or dogs apart from Flossie, but no one could fail to adore this little chap. He pranced on his spindly little legs, while his mother kept a careful watch over him

Amber held out her arms and gurgled. Eddy slipped between the rails, as he had obviously done before and ran over to WING. Micky seized Flossie as she made to follow. The foal allowed the child to stroke its neck, and then they chased each other as the mare looked on.

Micky, a little shamefacedly told me the story, While Mr Richard kept Raven he was not often used as a sire. When he was it was usually settlement of a gambling debt, and the foal went to the mare's owner. When Raven had again come under Micky's care, so near to death, he and Finch had brought him back to health. Micky rode him when he walked out. The horse would never hunt again, and seemed somehow sad without Mr. Richard. Micky chatted and cajoled Raven who now looked sleek with all the grooming and good food.

There could be only one solution – and here she was – a lively sixteen hand mare in full oestrus in his paddock one morning. As she trotted around looking over her shoulder with flaunted tail Raven planted himself in her path. It was not for a stallion of his standing to be chasing her! He looked her full in the eye, laid his head along her neck, and then with no resistance and a deal of encouragement did what stallions are supposed to do.

Clever Micky had waived a stud fee, so that Courtneys could keep the foal. He would also keep the mare until she would be returned to her owner again in foal. It was a splendid arrangement, and Raven never looked back when he could see the mare and his progeny from his stable or the next paddock..

Time flew by. Maggie Jones was confirmed as the new house manager. She listened attentively to what Bridie told her and kept copious notes. Soon Maggie took total control after shadowing Bridie, then they exchanged roles. Maggie had been both surprised and flattered to be offered such a responsible post outside her usual areas of expertise. However she was confident in her own abilities and accepted the challenge.

The wedding took place three days before Francis's arrival. Arabella had desperately wanted the reception to be held at Courtneys, but Dr. Daniels thought not!   Bridie had agreed to leave from Courtneys, spending the last night in one of the best guest bedrooms with Maire alongside her.   In the end they cuddled up together in the same bed as they had done as girls, and as sisters do.

They had spent a day in London buying bridal and bridesmaid outfits as a gift from Arabella.

All the staff lined up for Bridie to pass between them like the very important person that she was.   Then they sprinted for the charabanc, which was to spirit them to the church.   Their driver had to step on it to beat the wedding car, but they made it with minutes to spare.

Dr. Daniels looked distinguished, and Bridie delightful with flashing eyes and dazzling smile.   Maire followed her down the aisle looking demure and lovely.   They had both wanted Eddy and Amber as pageboy and tiny bridesmaid, but common sense and Dr. Daniel's 'Too young – there would be mayhem' prevailed. Thankfully there was no Nuptial Mass, and the guests piled back on the bus after nearly drowning the bride and groom in rose petals.   The reception was held at Bridie's new home, which proved to be perfectly appropriate and charming.   The bridegroom was his own man and Bridie would not have her own way in this marriage.   He insisted that as there was no 'father of the bride' he would provide the reception.   Bridie did manage to smuggle in extra champagne and beer.   Paddy had given her away so Liam and Micky were on drinks service.

Edmund Daniels never did find out why a few glasses of punch plus the beer and champagne rendered the guests so happy and jolly. He had obviously never tried 'Irish' punch before. He reasoned if this was a sample of his new married life, it was going to be quite lively!

So it had come at last.

Heralded by wedding and feasting then Amber's first birthday with all the excitement that brought to us all. There was the happiness of the reunion with Francis and the new realization that our reunions were wonderful, but our separations harder and harder to endure. He had much to tell me of our new home, and I tried so hard to be enthusiastic about it all. Our intimate reunion was as satisfactory as ever, we were undeniably compatible.

Then there were the constant decisions to be taken. Francis approved of Maggie Jones in her new post for she had impressed him immediately.

Finch at sixty-eight is ready for retirement but will be in charge until Maggie makes a new appointment. Since he spends so much time at the stables with Raven he may want to move into one of the apartments, so that the lads can keep an eye on him. There again it may be too much for him to leave his cottage and his mates at 'The Fox'.

The winter clothes trunks were all packed, and all my music would go with us. That at least should satisfy Francis of my intent. There were Amber and Nannie's trunks too. Maire had our summer trunks ready when the carrier came to collect them to be forwarded to Southampton. Only our travelling trunks remained to go to Southampton with us.

We had made our farewells on the previous day, and our gifts of gratitude. We had eaten supper in the library and spent our final summer evening in the famous summer house which had played such a vital role in our story.

We had made love for what felt like the last time in our lovely bedroom. I had fallen asleep wracked with the emotion of torn loyalties.

I rose early the next morning while Francis was still sleeping and toured my home.

I started with the great mural in the nursery where it all began when my father met my mother.

Each room held so many memories for me. I lingered especially in the Library and thought of dear Sir Edward, Sir Charles and Lady Cynthia; then the Great Hall where I had made my first singing debut. Finally in the Drawing Room where I had lighted so many fires and served so many trays of tea or coffee to the Courtneys and their guests. I leaned my head against the mantelpiece and burst into tears. It was then that I clearly heard my Mother's voice –
'COME ARABELLA- LIFE IS TO BE LIVED. GRASP IT WITH BOTH HANDS AND MOVE ON TO THE NEXT CHAPTER, MY BELOVED GIRL'.So it was that we left immediately after breakfast. All the staff – house, garden and stables were lined up to see us off and bid us farewell. Bridie, Eddy and even Dr. Daniels were there.

Finch stepped forward –.

"Ere it is at last Miss Arabella – you own named perfect rose.' I took it marveling at its colour and perfume. Overwhelmed I kissed my old Gardener on his knarled cheek and managed 'Oh Mr. Finch' before I choked up.

Maggie had handed me two letters. The first was a drawing of a black foal by Eddy and signed by all the staff wishing us 'Good Luck'.

The second was from Hugh Davenport – it read:-

'OPERA - NO

RECITALS - Perhaps NOT

A BROADWAY SHOW - Why NOT

Just keep singing I'll need you'

I smiled and waved as we drove off but I dared not look back.

So the future beckoned NEW COUNTRY NEW HOME NEW CAREER

I kissed my husband as we set off for New Horizons.

But for the first time ever Francis had forgotten to pack the portrait of the two children.

LM

ACKNOWLEDGEMENTS

The author gratefully acknowledges the huge help and encouragement given by:

ISOBEL COX

Brilliant at dates and information on America

VAL DE FAYE

Proof reader and so much more. Invaluable on tenses and time lines

HILARY FRYER

Ten flashing fingers and the ability to read my writing as volunteer typist

LUKE SMITH

Advisor on all things equine

DAVID SPILLER

A splendid help

PENNY WATTS RUSSELL

Able to produce any book or article on the same day as my enquiry

To all these technically adept friends a huge and heartfelt thank you.

Printed in Great Britain
by Amazon

68872429R00139